PRAISE FOR VIVIAN LIVINGSTON

"Vivian's popularity suggests that her followers, amid the attention they devote daily to work, family, and friends, may indeed find comfort in understanding the trials and successes of another ordinary woman."
—*The Christian Science Monitor*

"Vivian Livingston isn't a supermodel—she's a role model. . . . Vivian symbolizes the triumph of imperfection over perfection, for all women struggling with average bodies and often-problematic relationships, roommates, relatives, careers, coworkers, complexions, and menstrual cramps." —*San Jose Mercury News*

THE AUTOBIOGRAPHY OF VIVIAN

"Required Reading." —*Pages* magazine

"The funniest fictional heroine since Bridget Jones." —*Teen People*

The book is fodder for any woman who has dreams of living big despite humble beginnings." —*USA Today*

"Vivian's autobiography reads like a conversation over coffee with a long-lost friend. It is fun and sassy . . . and perfect for a sunny day at the beach or a rainy day on the couch." —*Booklist*

"If you're looking for a lighthearted, humorous book to dive into as you wade out the rest of summer, this novel screams your name. . . . You will not be disappointed." —*Las Vegas Mercury*

"Vivian's such a pal, and she's there for you 24/7 . . . Like having keys to a friend's place." —*Everett Herald*

VIVIAN LIVES

"Sherrie Krantz has done it again. If you loved her first book, you'll love this one. In my next life, I want to come back as Vivian. (If there is no 'next life,' then I definitely want to hang in heaven with Vivian!)"
—CAROL LEIFER, comedian, writer/producer of *Seinfeld*

Also by Vivian Livingston and Sherrie Krantz

The Autobiography of Vivian
Vivian Lives

ViViAN
The "V" Spot

by ViVIAN LiViNGSTON

AS TOLD TO SHERRIE KRANTZ

BALLANTINE BOOKS · NEW YORK

A Ballantine Book
Published by The Random House Publishing Group

www.ballantinebooks.com

Library of Congress Cataloging-in-Publication Data

Krantz, Sherrie.
The V spot : a novel / by Vivian Livingston as told to Sherrie Krantz.—1st ed.
     p.   cm.
ISBN 0-345-45356-5 (alk. paper)
1. Young women—Fiction. 2. Female friendship—Fiction. 3. Women
novelists—Fiction. 4. New York (N.Y.)—Fiction. I. Title.
PS3611.R37 V13
813'.6—dc22   2004041020

Manufactured in the United States of America

9 8 7 6 5 4 3 2 1

First Edition: July 2004

Text design by Susan Turner

For Nikki . . .

Acknowledgments

For their unparalleled love, support, and friendship, I thank my mom and my dad. They say you can't pick your family, but I am sure that I must have.

For my little brother, who, mysteriously, has taken on the role of a big one, I thank Sam Krantz.

For this entire adventure, which has touched so many people and has been one of the most important experiences of my life, I thank my editor, Allison Dickens.

For my small circle of friends and confidants, old and new, I thank you for bringing so much pleasure and so much clarity into my life.

And for everyone who has opened their arms and hearts to Vivian, our shared friend, I thank you for making me feel so connected to the rhythm of this world and for helping me understand my place in it.

prologue

So we meet again. . . . You look great. ☺ The third time is supposed to be the charm, right? So I should be all set for this third novel. I joke, of course. But really, these novels are becoming ritualistic, and its so exciting to begin this process again. I've missed you!

I want to say that I've come full circle, but that would have to mean my version of a circle and at this rate it's more of a pie than anything else, with a mysterious chunker of a slice missing!

Even weirder is the fact that I'm about to turn thirty, yes, you heard me. Astonishing, based on how immature, or better put, "young at heart," I am. So, it should come as no surprise that I'm still waiting for my bosoms to blossom into that full C I've been wishing for, having allotted a generous amount of time to an all-but-episodic stint in puberty! It's all about faith.

You'll begin to see how key my sense of humor is based on the "interesting" chain of events that take shape in this third novel. No author would be able to make this stuff up, I assure you.

So, with that, I think you should jump right in. A phrase very apropos as you will soon see. . . .

Enjoy, my sweets,

Vivian

ONE

Sure I'd heard of technology and mass transit but I'd be damned if I wasn't going to hand-deliver my first-ever manuscript into the palms of its true creator, Victoria Boz. After all, it was Victoria who had tapped me and bestowed the epitome of all gifts, a book deal.

Moments before, I slid into my favorite Madonna-slash-Missy-Elliott-inspired brown-slash-cream Adidas track pants, found a clean white Nike tank-slash-sports-bra, and Velcroed my black-slash-white Puma cross-trainers nice and tight. *What would I do without multi-purpose fashionable functional dress-down attire?* I thought. Contagious! (The days of my suitings and heels are so outnumbered!) Thankfully, I was able to snag a glimpse of myself just inches from my doorway and knew better than to go out in public with grouchy bed head galore. My trusty Kangol houndstooth cap was an earshot away, chillin' beside my big black *I'm-famous-fantasy* summer shades, and both rounded out my nouveau author attire quite nicely. It was almost noon and I had yet to go to bed the night before (I had finished my novel nearly three hours prior, eight forty-eight

A.M.), so the sunglasses were key unless I was going for the *I'm-a-crackhead* look.

My manuscript was pimped out as well, nestled inside a sharp bleeding-pink envelope I bought for about forty bucks at Kate's Paperie, the Barneys of the office supply world. This was my very first manuscript so I spared not a single expense! I was still sporting last year's carryall, an oversized Prada bowling bag (another from the Sophie Fashion Philanthropic Society), and it made the perfect sleeper for her. (My novel—I can't help but anthropomorphize her.)

Perhaps if I had calculated the trek beforehand, I may not have made such an impractical decision, but I do love a good walk, er, hike, even if it is hot as balls outside (hey, excuse the language, but when New York City is hot, unexpectedly brutally hot, there really is no expression better suited—trust me on that!), and this all really was a first.

My little defining moment was cursed from the beginning, I suppose, for when I arrived at Victoria's office, her assistant, Stephanie—with an attitude like a Fiona Apple record, a face that could be mistaken for the latest Gucci girl's, and a ruched black satin top that even I recognized from a current ad campaign—told me flatly that Victoria was in a do-not-disturb-under-any-circumstances meeting and I was instantly and uberly crushed.

"Just drop it in her in box," Stephanie murmured as she went back to an evidently more important conversation about lip gloss with her invisible friend through her earpiece. Easily a snarky suggestion that could only come from a girl who knew she didn't need to be nice to get far. Beyond being ridiculously stunning, her grandfather or grandmother or something was a best selling sci-fi writer. Unfair certainly but true for sure.

Trying to be agreeable, I glanced beyond her and saw this inbox thing. It was already overstuffed and hanging off the top right corner of Victoria's desk, like a drunk in stilettos, and I just couldn't bear to leave "her" there. (A feeling probably similar to a parent dropping her kid off with a babysitter who mentions "rehab" when you ask if she's had a nice summer.)

It was then that I realized that maybe, just maybe, only my tiny world revolved around me. 'Cause this so wasn't the way it was supposed to go! Where was the marching band, the champagne, the tissues, the collective awe at her size and her promptness???

Deep Breath.

I decided to buck Stephanie's unreliable system and leave my manuscript on Victoria's chair. I attached a Post-it (which also killed me) that read:

V—
She's shy . . . not ready for the in-box.
Read her and weep.
XO,
V

I briefly took in the moment for all its sights, sounds, and smells. I wanted to remember it forever. The aroma of the ink from a multi-paged fax coming in; the heat steaming from the hard drive of her computer, which must have been on for months. The endless books scrunching into every and any free inch of her nine-tiered bookshelf. The screaming teenagers. (Her office overlooked the MTV *TRL* studio in Times Square.) The few photos of her cat and my book cover, laid out on her desk waiting for her approval. Sa-sa-sa-real!

Unhappily interrupted, I noticed Stephanie spinning around in her chair, quickly checking up on me I suppose, and then rolling her eyes as she spun back still yapping. She carefully placed her can of Crush (yup—another girl who looks like that and gets to drink liquid sugar beverages!) arm's length away, maintaining a spillage safety zone, and I was immediately inspired.

I walked out of Victoria's office and tried as best I could not to stage a faux sneeze, but then:

"I saw you place that package on Victoria's chair, *Vivian* . . . ," she quipped, not even bothering to look my way and instead staring at her computer screen, focusing in on a very important instant message as though she were on to my deviant ways and too many miles above me to care, stop, and do anything about it. And then, I just couldn't help myself—

"Ex-ex-ex-SNEEZE-me!" I sneezed, flailing my left arm just enough to tip Mr. Crush right on his ass . . .

"Oh my God! Aim, I *have* to call you back!" she squealed and threw her headset off as rapidly as she would have gestured away a storm of bees.

"I'm so sorry Stephanie!" I gushed as the orange syruplike soda inched its way over her desk, poisoning everything in its way, like a pit viper that was on my team.

"I'm so sure," she barked as I skipped through the hallway and pressed the little elevator arrow for DOWN.

Once out of the building and back on the pavement that was still so freakin' hot, I was sure the rubber in the soles of my shoes would melt and literally stick me there, I left Victoria a voice mail:

Beep. "V, it's me. My baby is resting on your chair waiting for your tender loving care and seriously, I don't care how many books her ancestor has sold, we really need to find you a new assistant. This time it was soda. I can't be held responsible for what could happen next. Call me." *Beep.*

It was weird. Once I flipped my phone off I truly had no idea what to do with myself. My ridiculous handbag was now as empty as my head. I had nothing to worry about, no deadline to meet. I had taken a short temporary leave of absence from work, two weeks, to ensure the finished product. And I was early—three days. But it wasn't the oddity of not having a single physical duty; it was the space in my head. My brain was like an open pasture and maybe/maybe not due to the sun, two cute European kids in lederhosen each carrying a sunflower in an open hand were skipping through said pasture . . . 'cause that's how wide and open it was, not a single thought, plan, action item—nothing. And evidently, that's how lucid, exhausted, and dehydrated I was, well, you get the picture . . . right?

Kids in lederhosen???

Okay, anyway—the point is—it felt foreign to be so free.

I had spent the last eight months slaving over this novel. Torturing myself for the first four. Unable to type a single letter, never mind word, never mind sentence on my computer. If the light emitted from my desktop possessed even the slightest UV ray, honestly, I'd look like Venus Williams right now. I was sickened by the thought of anyone reading it. Wondering why I even thought I could do it in the first place. And then there were the critics . . .

Oosh.

Night after night, up till dawn, munching on carrots and dried cantaloupes till my skin turned orange. Sipping endless Tabs through straws until my esophagus burned. Rushing to work, late every day. Out of my mind and stuck in my head. Gaining weight by the second, losing years by the day. The stress of it all! Would it be worth it?

All the while, and very honestly, never thinking about Jack and what had happened. Disinterested in everything in the now, always focused on my past. For *The Autobiography of Vivian . . . a Novel* would be my story from college graduation until my foray onto the 'Net. So if it wasn't relevant to my moonlighting gig as an author, well, I was fully uninterested. Hence, strained friendships and less and less contact with the outside world. And no boys, not a single kiss, not a touch, for eight-plus months. Scary, right? I was beyond focused. I was obsessed.

So right now, on the street corner, the book wrapped, well, it felt alien to be a person again.

"I'll be right here."

(*E.T.* reference BTW.)

And that was just in the first few minutes!

I headed for the corner and hailed myself a cab. I wanted to go home and sleep a thousand sleeps. As we made our way downtown, I stared at my cell phone. Who to call? Who to call *first*?

Jack.

Pathetic, huh?

I hadn't spoken to the guy since, well, since *then*. (If you don't count the few phone calls coordinating drop-offs and pickups of each other's personal effects.) And that's when it hit me. When I knew it was over. 'Cause I couldn't call him. No way. It was then, purely, that I realized I had lost my best friend. I'd never mourned my decision not to marry him, and because of the book, I didn't allow myself to miss him. But when I had accomplished the biggest thing in my life, it was Jack that I wanted to share it with, *first*.

Sad.

Immediately, I ignored the pang in my heart and rushed to re-move the thought from my mind.

Sophie.

I dialed, first the office—voice mail. Next, her cell—voice mail. Finally, her apartment—voice mail.

Grrrrrrrrrr.

Mom.

Same deal.

Joseph.

Same deal.

May.

Same deal.

This was really starting to suck.

Where was everyone?

I hadn't a clue.

That's how removed I was. Gone were the days of keeping tabs. After a little while of not returning calls, participating with only one eye open and one ear shut, missing birthday parties and bailing from twice-rescheduled dinners organized on my behalf, my nearest and dearest had gotten the hint, I guessed. It was as if I were travel-ing the globe these past months and "no news was good news" where my loved ones were concerned.

Not to worry, I thought, I'd pick up where I left off.

Just, please, let me take a nap first.

Not so fast . . .

Anyone who thinks that life will take a load off and hang out till you're ready is, like I said, living in a fantasy world.

(Where kids wear lederhosen apparently???)

two

Assimilation was first and foremost on my to-do list. Reconnect with the world around me and above all else, find my place in it. The novel was done, edited, proofread . . . the whole nine. It would soon take on a life of its own and I needed only to accept it. I had created something and had just set it free and instead of waiting, worrying about the rush of realties and reactions, it was high time I got my groove on.

Allow me to share my "Postnovel To-Do List":

1. Assimilate.
2. Meet Sophie's new beau.
3. Lose "book weight" (twelve pound-a-roos).
4. Forewarn all necessary parties of the contents of novel.
5. Find some fun.
6. Kiss and be kissed.

7. Figure out a way to mark this time-slash-achievement.

8. Start working on *Book 2*.

I took my three remaining days off and cleaned house. Edited my closets, vacuumed my apartment, cleared out my fridge, organized my medicine cabinet, caught up on my bills, tore through my e-mails, cleaned my slipcovers . . . the works.

After all that was behind me and I'd swear my apartment was sparkling, I went to town. First I dropped Omelet off at the groomer (still a ritual nightmare), and once that frenzy was under control, I made best efforts to awaken the girl in me. I got a mani-slash-pedi and wax (everywhere); got my hair trimmed and my color done; bought new makeup and undies. (I take great pride in my Cosabella collection. I have every single color!!! I'm not bragging, I'm just a dork. How I went from stamps and Beanie Babies to mesh thong underwear is a mystery . . .) I stopped by Tower Records to update my CD collection and bought a new shower curtain just for fun. (Is it me or does a new shower curtain not make us renters out there feel like we've redecorated?)

Bags in tow and feeling like a chick straight out of a shampoo commercial, I skipped, er, traipsed is more like it, through Soho to see and be seen. (If that's not a first-rate assimilation attempt, I don't know what is.) Having not taken into consideration that I am a working-class girl with working-class friends, though, my big social-butterfly scheme turned out to be a flop. We "real women" don't seem to fraternize between the hours of nine and five on a weekday—not yet anyway!

With Omelet not ready for another few hours, I thought it would be fun to visit The Figaro, my old haunt. After all, it was nearby, and it had been two years easily since I had even seen the place. Having just penned a novel that revolved around my past adventures, one of which was my many many days as a waitress at this fine establishment, I thought it fitting to bring my memories to fruition.

I found great pleasure sitting at a table in what was my old section and hoped that a few of my former comrades would surface. But in what amounted to probably five or so minutes I realized that only the name of the place and the seating chart had stayed the same. From the menu to the awnings, the staff, the pulse—everything screamed *new ownership*, and I couldn't have been more disappointed. Immortalized only in the pages of my book, my home away from home had picked up and left, and I felt robbed. As though my history and the history of my beloved friends, from the busboys to the bartenders, the guys in the kitchen to the girls in the back—our experience had vanished. Erased like a phrase from a chalkboard, never to be seen again. There was barely enough left to trigger a nostalgic notion, and before I could hear their specials I was back on my feet and off to who-knows-where.

For some reason it's okay when we move on. But when the spaces that house our memories follow suit, time, in this strange passive-aggressive way, fully lets us know who's in control.

Bugger.

I walked east and through Greenwich Village. A part of the city that completely brings me back to my first days here. Tousled, raunchy, artistic, chaotic. Sprinkled of course with a few Starbucks and Gaps every once and again, but safe from developers, yuppies, and yogurt shops. At least for now.

As I made my way through cavalcades of NYU students and pockets of tourists, a tattoo parlor emerged in the distance. A few steps later I'd inadvertently stopped in front of its window, just missing a phone call from Sophie—finally!

I rested my things, tied my shiny new hair in a knot, and phoned in to hear her message:

Beep. "Viv, it's me . . . I'm so happy for you girl. I can't believe you finished it!!! Does this mean I get my best friend back? If you don't let me read it I am going to disown you—I mean it this time. Okay, so Rob is taking me to the Hamptons this weekend. We're leaving right after work. I can't believe you haven't met him yet! But Sunday night, if we beat the traffic, it's me, you, Omelet, and whatever's on HBO. Love you girl." *Beep.*

Hmmm. Guess it was time to break out Plan B. Wait, I didn't have one.

As I picked up my things and got ready to motor, four girls, definitely under sixteen, basically ran me over. They were leaving the tattoo place, staring at their newly ringed navels, and I, obviously, failed to register in their periphery.

"Fuck," one said.

"Sorry ma'am," apologized another one.

Ma'am???

I looked around.

She couldn't have been talking to me?

Enter: big burly bald guy with a ring through his nose, in a sleeveless Harley Davidson black T-shirt, paint up and down both arms, and a red-white-and-blue sweatband on his wrist. "She wasn't talking to me," he laughed and bluntly chucked his cigarette butt into the wind.

Huh?

"Hey, wait!" I urged as he turned to step back inside the place. But he ignored me.

Would someone mind telling me when I went from me to ma'am? I thought.

With my world rocked, I put my stuff back on the ground, undid my hair, shifted my body weight to one side, and, with my hands on my hips, checked out my reflection in the window.

I was no "ma'am"—I mean please!

Shifting my weight to the other side and oblivious to who might be witnessing me striking pose after pose, I continued taking a personal inventory while I silently talked myself off the ledge those little mall rats had just put me on.

"Hey Giselle!" I heard the Village People guy bark. "You're distracting my technician. Pout and puss in front of someone else's shop. You dig?"

Youch.

"Geez man," I said, "what's your problem?"

"From the looks of things, ma'am, it's you who's got the problem."

Oh great, I thought, *how profound. I'm being analyzed by that?* (But before I could get too ticked or dare to care about his assumptions, I had to smile. I was so reminded of the scene in *Ferris Bueller's Day Off* where Charlie Sheen meets Jennifer Grey at the police station. Am I not right??? Think back or rent it if you have to.)

"Whatever," I mumbled as I tried to downplay the smirk that was still smirking across my face, remembering one of my all-time favorite flicks! (And besides, *Whatever* was the best I could come up with.)

Fully ignoring him, I took once last quick glance at my reflection until . . .

"Whatever? That's the best you got?" he snickered.

Interrupted, annoyed, and a little grumpy I quipped, "Take it easy, all right?"

"Sure." He dismissed me for a moment but then continued, chuckling a bit, "You want ink?"

Huh?

"Come again?"

"A tattoo. Can't make up your mind? Is that it?"

Enter eyebrow raise here.

A tattoo?

Yes, I wanted a tattoo. I had always wanted a tattoo. I mean, haven't we all? But I was there merely by coincidence . . . I hadn't opened my tattooed can of worms in a while. A long while.

My tattooed dreams were cannibalized on more than one occasion. Growing up, my father would have none of it. To the point that even the lucky Cracker Jack prize tattoos were forbidden. And I remembered pleading with Jack to come with me one random rainy Saturday years before. I was ready. I wanted it and I wanted it right then and there. But Jack was unyielding. He had gotten one back in high school. A small peace sign on the left side of his lower torso that he hated, so he would not sympathize. I remember being so annoyed. As if because he had regrets, I would, too. I reminded him that he'd been drunk when he'd gotten his. That he went with his then girlfriend, a wannabe granola chick whose father owned half of Staten Island. They had gotten them together after a Dead show, same tatt same spot. But he wouldn't budge. After a short argument my buzz was killed and I moved on.

"We don't bite in here ya know," he coaxed. "Why don't you come in . . ."

I wasn't too sure. He looked a lot like a biter.

Curious, I picked up my things again and followed him in. I had time to kill and the heat outside was pretty brutal, so . . .

And sure enough, before I knew it, I was lost in the hundreds of images tacked up to the walls. Adding to the thrill were the lyrical stylings: Guns N' Roses blaring from speakers perched high in the four corners of the ceiling.

I felt bad, I felt good, and I felt rebellion a-brewin'!

As my eyes passed over every sailor-emblazoned epigram, Asian symbol, nautical theme, fifties naked pinup girl, and the rest I'm sure you can imagine, I embraced the unexpected and started weighing my rationale.

Was it a sign that I had stopped in front of a tattoo parlor, of all places?

- *I wanted to do something radical to commemorate this time in my life.*

- *I had always wanted a tattoo—the art and spot picked out a decade and a half before. (A license plate of roses, if you care to know.)*

- *And if I had indeed hit "ma'am-dom," then it*

surely didn't make a bit of difference whether I
had parental approval or not.

Yes, no, yes, no, yes . . .

"Tell me." I turned. "Is there anyone here who does custo—?"

"Nick" he fired out before I could finish my sentence. "Yo! Nick!"

And seconds later a guy whom I assumed was Nick emerged from the back. He looked like a cross between Colin Farrell and Iggy Pop. Long and lean, sporting flip-flops, a shrunken navy long-underwear top, tattered tan vintage cords cut off at the bottom, shredding just so and held up by a brown leather belt with a tarnished bronze circle as the buckle.

Helloooooooooo Nick!

He was so hot, you guys, it was like a moment out of a music video. Instead of seeing stars and fireworks, I could swear that our shared space became smoke-filled in what amounted to a heartbeat. He motioned toward me slowly. He parted seas. He moved mountains. The cat walked on water—that's how hot he was. It was a little trippy actually, but remember, it had been many a many months!!!

Now he, er, this, absolutely was a sign!

I was so definitely doing this. Right here, right now.

"Hey," he said and stretched out his arm to shake my hand. "Waz up? I'm Nick."

"Yo," I said, momentarily distracted because I couldn't believe I'd just said *yo.*

"You looking for somethin' special?" he asked.

I said nothing. His gorgeous green eyes were momentarily distracting.

"You want ink?" he tried again, leaning down a little, getting a close look at my eyes, maybe making sure I wasn't on anything. And much slower this time. Deciding between drugs and a severe learning disability, I gathered.

The "v" spot

His mouth was grand—took up the majority of his face—in a great way—no worries.

"Hey—uh—do—you—speak—English?"

"Uh-huh."

"You want a tatt, then?"

"Yup."

"Cool," he responded, somewhat relieved. "Do you know what you want?"

"Ab-so-lute-ly."

three

It wasn't more than sixty seconds before I was on the phone with the groomer, giving them my credit card number and requesting that Omelet be dropped off at my apartment. Next I rang my neighbors (think *Queer Eye for the Straight Guy*—two well-groomed guys who couldn't wait to reinvent me and my apartment) asking them to let Omelet in. When I clicked my phone closed I had already entered what felt more like a dungeon than a studio. The space was dark, lit only by an aging halogen lamp. Assorted graphic neon dorm-room-esque posters adorned, from what I could tell, the wall, and now it was Metallica that was hurling through the air.

My eyes then met an operating-table-looking fixture in the center of the small small room. It looked a lot like a reject from my pediatrician's old office. A table that I assumed I was meant to lie on. Its texture reminiscent of faux leather—the kinda thing that was stain resistant—stain resilient more likely.

Before my better judgment could set in, Nick removed his shirt— "It's real hot in here, ya know. You don't mind, do you?"

"Oh no, not at all." I blushed. (*Take it all off* was my next thought.)

I was quite surprised to see that little Nick was tatt-less. But as my eyes scrolled up, down, around, and across this man of a man, I did notice the two words carved into his knuckles—Ozzy style.

One hand read: DEATH.

The other: NEVER.

???????????????

He noticed me noticing and, I gather, felt the need to explain:

"It's just a reminder to myself . . . you know?"

"Not really," I admitted.

"See: NEVER [placing his first fist inches from my face] back down."

"Uh-huh," I said, feeling as boring and "ma'am-y" as you might imagine.

"And DEATH [again with the fist] like—*I'm gonna die one day, any day, so I've got to live in the moment . . .*"

He stood silent after delivering those words, awaiting and probably expecting my response.

"Cool" was, again, all I could come up with.

A little EXTREME if you ask me, I thought. *But. I get it.*

"So anyway." He moved on. "What are you thinking? And where?"

I propped myself up onto the "examining table" as awkwardly as you might expect. (It had been ages since my shoulders and triceps had been properly worked out.) My butt, can't leave this out, had to act like a bumper—the peak-slash-top hitting the edge of the table as though it were the bumper of a car. On the bright side, the redness from the eventual bruise would make for a no-miss bull's-eye as far as tattoo location was concerned.

Finally perched atop, with my feet several inches off the ground, I slid my sneakers off, praying that they didn't reek, and placed my phone and bag by my side. "I've always wanted roses," I said. As shy as I was revved up to be moments away from scarring my body for life.

"Nice," he encouraged.

"Thanks," I said, batting my eyelids like a young deer in a Disney movie.

"So what size were you thinking, how big?"

"I always sort of saw it being kinda big actually," I explained. "If we went too small, I doubt you'd be able to make out what the flowers were, ya know."

"Uh-huh."

"Oh, and also"—I was getting into this—"I want the colors to be really bright and happy—colorful. Not typical tatt colors—very girly."

"Sweet."

"Oh, and one more thing. No outline. Well, I mean, an outline of course, but not black and dark. I don't want the outline to take away from the detail."

"Sure thing. It's pretty cool—you know what you want, I like that. I mean . . . can I be honest with you?"

"Sure."

"If one more girl comes in here and wants to get one of them Nemo dolphin things on her ankle I'm gonna quit and go back to . . ."

"Yeah?"

"Back to, um . . ."

"Yeah," I said. "Back to . . . what?" (Medicine, I hoped!)

"Well, just back. I'd quit. I'd walk."

"I see," I whispered, somewhat disappointed.

He broke out a sketchbook and started doing roughs of the roses. And he had me pick out some colors from swatches he had attached to what I thought to be a key chain.

There was silence for a few, which I'm sure I was the only one to find a bit awkward. In my mind, my subconscious really, this was our "first date," and Nick wasn't exactly a chatterbox.

But then . . .

"This is what I went to art school for," he peeped. "Everyone thought I was crazy, taking out loans, dropping all this cash for an education, so that I could move to New York and become a tattoo artist. But . . . I'm fixin' to open my own place one day."

There it is, I thought—*a plan. Me like-ee.*

"I don't think that's crazy," I said, supporting my soon-to-be new boyfriend's dream.

He revealed his sketchbook and I more than loved what I saw.

"That's it!" I yelped. "That's it!" I made a few *Nutty Professor* Eddie-Murphy-inspired, *Hercules* mini clap gestures and giggled, forcing myself to keep my uncoolness caged for as long as humanly possible.

"Rad," he said, nodding in agreement, slowly, as though he were listening to music.

I jumped off the table to get a better look.

"Get back up there," he chuckled and quickly scooped me back into position.

☺

"So where is this going?" he asked.

"Right around . . . here," I said. Twisting myself around, feeling for my panty line, which of course was sticking out anyway. "Just below there."

"That's hot," he said, sounding very much like Jeff Spicoli from *Fast Times at Ridgemont High.*

"Ya think?"

"Totally . . . it's stripper hot."

Um. Okay—enter: second thoughts.

Nick had ESP, evidently, and soon realized that *stripper hot* was not quite the look I was going for. "You know what I mean," he corrected himself. "It's just hot."

Quite a way with words, this one.

Knowing that the tattoo would never appear above my jeans or undies or bathing suit, I took the high road and stayed put. I was doing this for me. A statement for myself. Something I'd wanted for-ever and ever and it was time to put my money where my mouth was, along with my obvious desire to feel young and a little out of control—no ma'am—not near—but far. Very very far.

He asked me to unzip my pants, pull them down as far as I felt comfortable, and sit Indian style with my back to him. Then he asked if I wanted anything to drink.

"Vodka," I said, my tummy already regretting my decision.

"No no no . . . I've got water, tea, soda."

"I'm good—let's just get on with it." I took a deep breath and held it as though a cemetery were passing before me.

"You've got to breathe, Jillian," he said.

"Vivian," I whispered, tersely.

"Of course," he apologized. "My bad . . . Ya ready? Vivian. Vi-vian. Vivian."

Another movie moment, sorry—but I couldn't help but think of Nick Nolte, as Tom Wingo, in the last scene of *The Prince of Tides* . . . driving over the bridge into the sunset thinking of Barbra Streisand . . . "Lowenstein, Lowenstein, Lowenstein." Beyond bittersweet.

Ahhhhhhhhhhhhhh.

FUUUUUUUUCCCCCCCCKKKKKKKK!!!!

four

hat followed was four-plus hours of TORTURE.

In just the first second I was filled with regret. As the Metallica wailed, each time I caught a glimpse of Nick's freakishly inked knuckles, I felt more and more like a poseur with a serious identity disorder.

There was even a moment, no wait, two, when my legs went numb and I visualized myself, outfitted in a wheelchair, lecturing to students about the dangers of tattoos.

"Can I see?" I begged.

"Nope."

"You sure?"

"Yup."

Ugh.

Making matters worse, besides the significant sweating and the rushes of panic that were wreaking havoc on my nervous system, Nick's little alcove held the shop's single fully functioning lavatory, so he was constantly being interrupted, having to start and stop over and over again. Would my roses turn out to be weeds?

And with one "Sorry man but I gotta go" character after another, pierced through the nose, through the lip, through the eye-brow, with black fingernail polish and/or a shellacked gravity-ignor-ing Mohawk, iridescent dyed hair, platform patent leather shoes, or scuffed-up burgundy Doc Martens high-tops, I couldn't help but feel ridiculous.

Desperate for something familiar and moments from passing out, I pleaded with Nick, "Hey, um, could you see if they can play any Britney in here?"

"Honestly, I'd be afraid to ask." He chuckled. "Hang in there, cutie, I'm almost done."

Ahhh, *cutie*, and the whole time I'd thought his bedside manner sucked.

And Nick wasn't kidding because minutes later, silence en-sued. The patchy Morse-code drumming of the apparatus used to apply the tattoo died away. I heard that switch sound, sound off, and then the little room possessed only the vibrations of their never-quitting sound system. And of course there was the sound of pain, the beating and pulsing of my skin, but that, I was sure, was de-tectable only by me.

I turned, shifting my body, slowly, in Nick's direction, and I quickly saw my reflection, shoulders to torso, through the mirror that he was holding in his hand.

He made the mistake of giving me my care-for and "preven-tive" instructions in those next few moments, which were so filled with pain and anticipation that everything he said went in one ear and out the other one at lightning speed.

"You've got to let me see it now, Nick. I'm serious," I said, di-rectly. And with that, he helped me to my feet and guided me toward a full-length mirror that had been hiding behind the bath-room door all this time. Even the *thought* of standing upright and staring straight ahead exhausted me, so I maneuvered, snail-like and slightly hunched over, focusing on our shared hands. As I stared at his knuckles yet again, they and he seemed surprisingly different.

I felt camaraderie in a rite of passage that before was only isolating. A slight optimism trailed me as he unveiled my tattoo.

He turned me around (think "Pin the Tail on the Donkey") and placed the smaller mirror to allow a perfect view of my new and improved derrière.

But I wouldn't look. I squeezed my eyes together, shutting them, nervous beyond nervous.

"Oh, come on now, Vivian, you're hurting my feelings. Have you no faith," he said warmly.

"I just can't believe I actually did it . . . What if I don't like it? What then?" I whimpered, like a five-year-old who doesn't want to go to bed.

"It's hot. You're gonna love it. Now suck it up and get a-lookin'."

I opened one eye, and although things looked fuzzy, I couldn't help but grin. It was an *I-cannot-believe-I-actually-went-through-with-it* grin, and that small sense of accomplishment erased any remaining fears. And like a blue streak both my eyes were open, and voilà, there she was, and I'm telling you guys, I LOVED IT!

I couldn't believe that I was looking at me. I just stared and focused, wanting to appreciate every detail.

"So?" Nick said, impatiently. "Are you gonna say anything?"

"I love it, Rick. I love it!"

"It's Nick," he said with a smile, a great smile.

"Yeah, I know." I was, still staring at, well, at me. "I'm just messing with you."

five

On my way to work that fol-
lowing Monday I felt wildly optimistic. My bandaged backside was
no longer; I had nothing but my nine-to-five to worry about, and it
was one of those Mondays where the world felt like my oyster.

I had spent the evening before with Sophie, perfectly bronzed
and perfectly in love; she was an inspiration. It was heavenly to sit
beside her again, focused, listening intently to all the scoop she
served up. (And yes, I let her read my book. Er, some of it. Well, just
the prologue and chapter 1—it's too embarrassing!) And this Rob
guy, well, he sounded like a dream and I had never seen her so
calm and sure of herself. (Could this be the rumored glow of a
healthy relationship?)

They had been together for only three months, but she was sure
he was "it." That's when I instinctively poured myself a glass of wine.
This was the first time I'd heard Sophie say such a thing and really believe it. He was older, born and raised in the city, he was (very) successful, a stockbroker who'd gotten in and out of a few significant
'Net stocks at just the right time. And evidently—and this is a big one
for Soph—he was a wicked dresser! What did she love most about

him? Well, she had a list and just at top, front, and center was this *my girl* thing that he did . . .

For example, "Is *my girl* just not the most beautiful girl in the world?" and "Look at *my girl*, God, she's the best."

Okayyyyyyyyyy.

There we sat. Me in Jack's tattered original eighty-something Rolling Stones official black concert T-shirt that I simply couldn't give back, a pair of dirty white Paper Denim and Cloth stretched-out jeans, barefoot with black bottoms, yesterday's mascara, and my hair in a pony that I did not look forward to trying to take out. And "Sandra Dee" here. As comfy and as cozy as you could possibly imagine, sitting Indian style in a baby-pink terry Juicy Couture sweat suit, perfect makeup, and a hint of some fruity perfume. Straight-ironed bleached-blond hair with sun-kissed streaks arithmetrically scattered about, and one huge smile waiting to happen that would escape between her sentences. As she continued citing one amazing "Rob attribute" after another, I canvassed her. Even her French-manicured toes looked jubilant. Her gold Grecian sandals were opulent. Her tanned shiny skin ecstatic. The golden diamond-encrusted huggies that did indeed hug her edible earlobes were beaming, too. We couldn't be more different if we tried and trust me here: You didn't need to be some hugely annoying *CSI* fanatic to detect it. (I'm Jo, she's Blair. One of those simple and true *Facts of Life*.) I couldn't help but shake my head as she interrupted with a "What?"

"It's just . . ."

"What?" She giggled again.

"You're just . . ."

"What?" Now a laugh.

"Adorable!!! I mean who are you???"

She giggled, ecstatically. "I'm just so happy, Vivi!"

"I know!" I said, half chuckling, half choked up.

We hugged each other until I felt a slash of pain run up my back. "Yooouch!"

"What is it, Viv?"

"Nothing."

I didn't want to interrupt her moment and besides, I was taking crucial mental notes. Her happiness was a foreign thing. Sure, I knew tons of people who described the whole "in-love" concept and who were in great relationships, but Sophie's was different. My best friend was going through it, and I knew her deal inside and out. Her history, her fears, her Cinderella story that, up until now, needed only the Prince Charming. How did it happen? When did it happen? How did she really know? Did this guy love her for all the reasons he should—all the reasons I knew someone would? All the things that the others before him took for granted or ignored? And more importantly, did he have any friends???

Sophie was full of surprises that day. In addition to looking like Kate Hudson's long-lost sister, she was tossing around the idea of quitting her job and traveling with Rob for the next few months.

"He thinks I could get another job in a heartbeat, V, and he wants me with him, so I'm taking it pretty seriously. I mean, a month in Los Angeles, a few weeks in Tokyo, and then Thanksgiving in Rome???"

Her eyebrows on automatic pilot, she was waiting for my response. I could only assume that Sophie was looking to me as her voice of reason, because we girls know that love is a wee bit distracting.

"I don't know, Soph . . ."

"Bad idea?" she sighed disappointedly.

"No, not a bad idea . . . It's a CRAZY idea. It's an amazing idea," I said.

She perked up. "But . . ."

"But, God, it's been what? Three, maybe four months? Do you think quitting a job you love, giving up an apartment that you and I both know is impossible to come by, and above all else leaving me all by my lonesome is the right thing to do?"

She nodded, adorably.

"Well . . . [pause] then do it!!!"

33

We laughed again and hugged again and then I "youched" again.

Puzzled, concerned, she was on to me. "What is the deal with you, Viv?"

"Nothing," I said with a smirk.

"What's going on back there? What are you hiding?"

"Nothing," I said, getting up from the couch, slowly.

"Did you—"

"No, Sophie, it's nothing, really," I tried insisting.

"Did you?"

"It's nothing Soph!"

"Oh my God, V, did you . . . get liposuction???"

HUH?

"What?" I shouted defensively. "You think I . . . Oh my God, NO!"

"Relax, okay?" she said sternly. "I mean, what am I supposed to think?"

"What are you supposed to think? Hell, I don't know, maybe I have a backache? Maybe I hurt myself lifting something? Maybe I'm premenstrual!!!"

"Take it easy! You're scaring Omelet!" She laughed.

I looked. He wasn't scared. Annoyed, maybe, but definitely not scared.

I turned and made my way back to the kitchen but couldn't help but bellow, "Jeez, Sophie, just when I was learning to love my ass, you go and well, God . . . LIPOSUCTION?!?"

"Not participatinnnng!" she sang aloud. "Lipo-convo over!"

I responded with a huff and puff from the kitchen. This was the first hour, post-tattoo, that my appetite was back in full force. As I stood peering into what was, and almost always is, an empty pantry filled with nothing and more nothing, Sophie sneaked up on me and pulled my T-shirt up. And I was, for lack of better word, busted.

"Holy . . . I can't believe . . . I can't believe you fucking did it! I can't believe it! Get over here," she screamed, pulling at my already stretched-out T-shirt, leading me back and backward into my living room. "Get over here. Let me see her!!!"

"All right, all right. Hang on and get off!" I whined.

(Red wine now splattering on my hardwood floors.)

I stripped, then displayed my roses with pride.

"I, I, I . . ."

"Oh my God," I said nervously, "you hate her."

"Noooooooooo, I love her! She's gorg. She's hot, V. My God, she's hot! I want one!"

"Isn't she!" I said with pride and delight and now on my third glass of red wine.

I told her about the hell that had come with it, and she told me about the little dolphin that she was thinking about for her ankle. ☺

I didn't sleep much that night. It wasn't because of stress or pain or anything like that. I was just all over the place and a little lit, too. I thought back to the weekend Sophie and I spent here, more like the Christina Ag-u-scary-a look-alikes who had anointed me a "ma'am" than the women we are today. Before we graduated, that one crazy weekend we spent in New York City, when I just knew we had to pack it in and make the Big Apple our permanent residence. We had both changed so much since then but still so little. Sophie remained herself, just a different version. Simple, sweet, beautiful, happy-go-lucky, and helplessly carefree. I was still a mess. Accomplished, but a mess no less. As single as I was the day I'd stepped off the bus. As sensitive and neurotic as ever. I couldn't help but wonder if maybe that was MY THING. Where Sophie was always the little lady, groomed to the core with an infectious demeanor, would I always be the tomboy with the penchant for drama and an X in every corner of my mind? Was I the tortured soul and she the blithe spirit?

And who was this Rob person anyway? What was the story there? I had heard through the grapevine that he was in fact pretty great—but there had to be a catch. There always is. Isn't there???

Me and my tattoo were tired. It had been a long weekend. I let the knowledge that although time passes, it's pretty easy to catch up, cradle me as I counted back from a hundred trying to fall asleep. Sophie had always been my touchstone, and it was such a relief to know that a book and a boyfriend had not gotten in the way of what we shared. Not yet at least.

So like I said, I began this Monday with great hope that I'd find a happiness that was thorough. A tatt earned and without repercussions, a personal milestone finally reached, or something as inconsequential as a great hair day, together, couldn't measure up to what Sophie had been sporting. I knew that a balance was long overdue and I was fixin' to find mine.

six

Work seemed like a new place. While writing the book I'd been out of the office more than I was in it, and work was a bit foggy for a while. Motoring through the motions, doing the minimal, hightailing come quittin' time, and resenting any new business or projects 'cause they'd keep me from my commitment du jour (the book, of course!).

But now, it was like a new gig for me. Like a pair of brand-new shoes that I'd forgotten about for months. Coming across them in my closet after a season or two, still loving them, donning them proudly, eagerly, and introducing that contagious immediate-gratification-purchase feeling for a brilliant and unrealized second time.

I had been in the same job and at the same desk for almost four years but it felt so new and so different now.

Most of the usual suspects were still suspecting: Sheryl, the head of publicity, didn't leave her house without a straightening iron, vitamins, and a *Laverne-&-Shirley*-inspired initialed garment of some kind. Marni, her now full-time assistant, a recent and young bride who was quickly becoming quite the little junior executive. May, now special projects manager, one of my closest confidantes, had earned her stripes big-time, as Stan's former assistant and, in my humble opinion, a real-life version of Halle Berry. Drew, our ad man, and my man-cocktail during office hours. (Read *Book 2*. Too long a story to get into.) And of course Stan, my boss whom I so love to hate. Think Simon Doonan sans any creativity and still locked in a closet. New hires: Angela—Stan's latest right hand—an earnest intern with blinders on who sees her new (paying) role as the ultimate challenge. (Best of luck sweetie.) Daniel—Drew's newest left—think clothed Abercrombie & Fitch catalog boy with a fine British accent to boot. (May, Sheryl, Marni, Angela, Jayden, and I sent Drew a thank-you card after that one.) And then there's Jayden, both of my hands. A bit rough-and-tumble like yours truly, from upstate New York, didn't know what she wanted to do when she moved to the big city, she just knew she "had to be here." Sound familiar???

See, in Corporate America, excuse me, Belaboring Suffering Corporate America, assistants are the gifts that keep on giving. They come much cheaper than, say, a fully staffed department, corporate perks, or uneven raises. So by hiring support staff, the company lets you know they care without having to loosen their belt buckles too much. A selfish gift. (It's kinda the same thing as when your boyfriend buys you *more* lingerie as a birthday present—sort of.) How are right-out-of-college-greener-than-Kermit assistants going to help you realize your corporate inititiatives and solve the problems of the business? Well, they aren't. BUT they do make your life a lot less miserable while coming to terms with that fact. And they also put more space between the day you find out you're getting one and the day you say *I quit!* So basically, Jayden entering my life, right around the time that I had to start moonlighting as an author, was a blessing.

I myself had been an assistant for a looooong time. Way longer than I had been a waitress. And even when I wasn't an assistant, it took a very looooong time for coworkers to acclimate and not treat me like one. So I vowed that the day someone worked for me, I'd try to be the best boss ever. I had never been fortunate enough to ever have someone allocated just to help me, so realistically this was pretty sweet. Plus I really liked Jayden, so working long hours with her was easy. She had a golden retriever named Captain and a long-distance beau in Seattle named Neal (yes, there is a joke there) and a penchant for carbohydrates that rivaled even mine. She was a good egg and a cool girl and I hoped she would one day think of me in much the same way I did my mentors from years past.

But before I go on, I should say this. I was lucky to even have my job and I always felt a pang of guilt when I bitched about it. It was now midway through 2002 and besides the uniqueness of my situation—i.e., www.vivianlives.com—lots of companies, especially Web-based companies, had vanished. So things could have been much worse. We were one of the last Web-based entertainment sites standing, and although I was frustrated with my job at times and the snail's pace at which the company was growing, we were, by definition and by comparison, doing "well."

Upon entering, my office looked like UPS and FedEx had taken over, or maybe had had a crazy party in it the night prior. Before I even thought to turn my computer on, I raised the blinds, slid open the window, ordered a coffee and a bagel with extra chive cream cheese, threw my blazer on my chair, flipped my pumps off, undid the button of my pants (remember I was sporting some extra poundage), got comfortable on my thankfully carpeted floor, and began to make sense of the chaos. Befitting my luck, Jayden had caught a nasty case and the adult version of the chicken pox, so of course she'd been out, along with me, and the mayhem was spilling over much like the unwelcome roll of my belly. We would share our first day back together.

"Look what the cat dragged in!" Sheryl proclaimed, appearing in my doorway, energy drink in one hand, *Variety, Advertising Age,* and *Women's Wear Daily* scrunched in the other.

"Hey stranger," I said.

"Hi author," she replied with a wink. "I'd better have been immortalized in that autobiography of yours . . . you should never forget the little people, you know."

Oops.

"How are you, Sheryl?" I smiled. "Have you been away?" She had the most incredible perfected Brazilian-looking tan I'd ever seen in my life!

"Pretty good!" she said rather chipperly. "I started Pilates and I looooove it."

"And—?" I said, still waiting for the Hawaiian Tropic explanation.

"Oh, and I started getting sprayed."

"Sprayed? As in insecticides? What do you mean, *sprayed*?" It sounded so ridiculous.

"Have you been living under a rock, V? Oh, wait a minute; you have actually, your novel. You're excused."

"Thanks," I said, relieved—not.

"My spa just got this new Los-Angeles-inspired tanning thing-ee. You get completely naked and they spray-paint you. Lasts ten days. Genius, right?" She twirled around. "How do you think J.Lo and Britney get their color? One day they're fair and all gamine and the next day, voilà, they're hot and healthy and trop-i-cal! Honey—you've got to come with next time!"

"Leave it to you, Sher," I said, while fighting with a mean TEAR HERE red indicator at the far edge of one of a thousand similar boxes all taking over my office!!

"Let Jayden handle all this, Viv." She waved a hand at the hurricane o' cardboard. "We're scheduled to be at Chelsea Piers in about thirty minutes."

"Excuse me?" I said. "Chelsea Piers? Are we going fishing?"

"You didn't get the message, I take it?" she quipped.

"What message?"

"Supreme Vodka . . . they're taking us on their yacht for the day. They're interested in you, the site, same thing, whatever, for advertising for next summer. Just a bunch of boys looking for an excuse to use their corporate perks. No big thing, and I brought lotion and an extra bikini so you're good to go!"

"Bikini? Ugh," I moaned.

Ever since *Jaws*, which was basically forever for me, I was fully afraid of the water. Pools didn't count and lakes, well, it wasn't sharks that I feared. Instead it was Loch Ness monsters. I like my rivers and oceans when I'm on vacation and I can have a buddy watching out for me—better still, a lifeguard—and where I can get back to the shoreline in ten, count 'em, ten paces.

Double ugh. (Had I been standing I would have stomped my feet.)

Plus, I was still on this pain medication for the tattoo and it was making me a little queasy. And I was hardly prepared for a day at sea. I mean, I was ten (okay, twelve) pounds over my usual weight, I had a tornado of a to-do list giving me dirty looks from my desktop, I had an assistant with a contagious disease, and I hadn't even had my coffee yet! This was all a sign telling me to stay put and keep busy until it was safe to go home.

Then, SMACK, a pigeon flew right into my window, the double-sided one, good for me, bad for the bird, and it nearly gave me a heart attack. God knows what befell the pigeon.

"Okay, Sheryl—that was definitely a sign!" I pointed up to my window from my floor.

"A sign? A sign of what?" she asked abruptly. The pigeon had scared her, too, and now her clothes and my carpet had enough nutrients seeping into them to last the whole day through!

"I can't go," I said quietly, fearing that *can't* was not a word Sheryl would accept.

Now using her morning literature to wipe off her doused outfit, she said, "Can't is not an option, V. Suck it up and I'll come get you in"—looking at her watch—"fifteen minutes."

Oye.

I looked up at my medium-sized stuffed Miss Piggy doll, seated next to my thesaurus, which was next to my signed glass-cased volleyball by none other than my athletic idol, Gabriella Reece herself, all resting atop my file cabinet, and pleaded with her to do something.

Nothing. (I think she's still pissed 'cause I gave up veal pretty easily but pork has been a whole other head game.)

Anyway, I got up and shut my door. Maybe someone would forget me here, think Tom Hanks in *Cast Away* . . . sorry for the lame analogy, but between the volleyball and the FedEx boxes it can't be helped!

Jayden via intercom:

J: *Vivian* . . .
Me: *Hi Jayden.*
J: *Do you have a second?*
Me: *Many.*
J: *Okay. 'Bye.*

Door opens and Jayden walks in.

"Hi," she said nervously.

"Hey," I said, feeling weird, only 'cause she seemed nervous.

"Sorry about your office. Had I been here . . ."

"No worries. How are you feeling?"

"Oh, so much better. Thanks!"

"Good. Chicken pox at five was hard enough. I can't even imagine—"

"Pretty brutal," she interrupted.

"Hey, you're pretty lucky. Doesn't look like they got to your face."

"What?" she said awkwardly, fidgeting with her hands—think Julia Roberts as Vivian before she got fancy in *Pretty Woman*. (Real quick: Was I the only preteen who tossed around the idea of being a high-priced call girl when I grew up after seeing that movie?)

"The pock-er-oos J," I reminded her. "As a kid it's cute when one lands smack on the center of your nose, as an adult, yikes!"

"Oh, right."

She just stood there.

"What's up?" I asked again. "Is everything okay?"

"Well, yes, kinda, no . . . yes, great, but no, not good."

My head trailed her to the point that my neck got sore. "Jayden, babe, what are you talking about?"

She joined me on the floor.

?

"I'm leaving," she said and gabbed my hand. Probably right after she saw my jaw drop and the shade of my skin go from olive to opaque.

"It's going to be okay, Vivian. Don't worry."

Huh? She's quitting, she's consoling me, and she's twenty-one. No wait, twenty-two, tomorrow. I hoped the gift I got her last week at Anthropologie was returnable. And not for store credit only—I hate when stores pull that shit.

"Vivian?"

"Sorry. Wait a second. You're quitting? When? Why? To do what? To go where?" I was suddenly paranoid. This was the first time anyone had ever resigned on me, to me. I took it personally.

"It's Neal. He wants me and Captain to move to Seattle. We're going to sell beaded—"

"Hang on, you're quitting to move across the country to sell beads with a guy you cheated on last week?"

"Shhhhhhh," she urged.

"No one can hear me, Jayden."

"I was drunk and he was real cute."

"Fine, whatever, that's beside the point." I was beginning to understand what being my mother must have been like. "When are you thinking? The fall? The spring? What?"

And then she said it . . .

"Two weeks."

Marni entered my office. "Hi Viv. Welcome back! Hey Jayden."

"Hi Marni," I mumbled.

"Hey Marn," Jayden said.

"Viv, Sheryl called a car for you guys. It will be here, downstairs, in a few minutes. Drew's going to meet you guys there. Car six sixty-six."

"Perfect," I groaned.

"Okay. 'Bye," she said and with that it was back to, uch, this.

"Can we talk about this later Jayden? I've got to do this boat thing. I should be back . . . hell, I have no idea when I'll be back. Just deal with—" I looked around the room. "—well, this, all of this, for me, okay?"

"Of course," she said sweetly, which basically just stung. She was great and what I thought to be irreplaceable and man was I bummed. I was hopeful, thinking that maybe I could talk her out of it, take her for a drink that night, see if perhaps Stan would approve a tiny raise, something. "Oh and Viv," she said, "I'm meeting with Human Resources at eleven to fill out some paperwork and then I was thinking of talking with a few friends. I really want to help you find a replacement."

Okay. Scratch Plan B. She definitely had her plane tickets.

"Viviaaaaaaaaaaaan!" bellowed Sheryl from down the hall. "Let's go!"

"Coming!"

Ugh.

Honestly, had Daniel not run down with my coffee and bagel just as we were set to jet and put a little smile into my first day back, I would have not been surprised if the Supreme sailing experience turned into a *Titanic* one.

Thank God for pretty boyz.

seven

Now in the car, I felt like Casper the Friendly Ghost next to Sheryl. I wasn't in the mood to sport my "game face"; nor did I feel like seeing Drew. My bra, which I'd accidentally put in the dryer the night before, and the only one that didn't show through the blouse I had on, was suffocating me. My tattoo was itching me worse than any nagging open mosquito bite ever could and my boobs, the only plus I can think of to gaining weight, were bursting out of my top, think Pamela Anderson and then take it down a notch or five. Bottom line: I was self-conscious and irritable and I pitied anyone who had to be around me.

"Come on now, Vivian, perk up, will you?" Sheryl urged.

"I'm trying, Sheryl, okay? I'm trying."

Insert: momentary awkward silence.

Biting the heads off friends-slash-coworkers is a trait I reserve typically for boyfriends and Stan.

"Sorry, Sher," I confessed. "I'm just a little overwhelmed."

"It's cool, Vivian."

"No it's not. I was just all pumped up to come back, get squared away, and then well, Jayden resigns—"

"Really?"

"Yup. And my office—"

"I know. I saw it. Frightening."

"And then this Supreme thing."

"It's fine, Vivian, really. You're a diva now." She laughed.

"Hardly," I said urgently.

"I can't wait to read your book! I'm freaking out!!!"

Ugh.

"No, really. I'm so excited for you. How many people can say that they wrote a book? That's the coolest thing. It'll be around for-ever and ever."

I shot her a *please-please-please-stop-talking-about-it* look and she got it.

"Moving on . . . ," she joked.

"So what's up with you, Sher? How have you been?" I asked curiously. Sheryl was always up to something.

"Well," she said coyly. "I met someone!"

"Really! Wow Sher, tell me."

Sheryl was a workaholic. I'd never heard her talk about a guy before. You could almost get the impression that she didn't need the TLC most women do. She was a self-starter with a blizzard of a social life and a girl with many passions—and then there was her work. Priority numero uno, since the moment we'd met. Always buzzing, always thinking, always maneuvering. Somehow I just couldn't figure how a boy could fit in.

"He's a fellow yogi . . ."

This made more sense.

"And he's kind and he's calm and unaffected and he's driven. He has a chain of studios on Long Island." You could tell she was just warming up.

"And . . . ?" I inquired.

"And, he's great Vivian. He's perfect!" Her cell phone started to ring and without looking to see who might be calling, she switched it right off. I did a double take. I had never seen her this way. She was so smitten. It was cute. She was distracted. She was, yes, a human being, too.

"Is it serious?" I asked.

"Very."

"How long?"

"About three months."

(What's with everyone and the "three months" by the way???)

"Why didn't you say anything? I can't believe you didn't tell me!" I whimpered.

"Look, Vivian, to me, boyfriends are like babies. You wait until the first trimester's over before you say anything . . . bad luck."

"Interesting," I said.

And it was. Made some sense. But what besides a fresh-out-of-the-microwave day-old Roy Rogers cheeseburger is better than revealing the beginnings of a "thing" to your girlfriends?!? Sheryl was a different breed, and her "trimester" theory all but proved it.

Before long we were there, the zone that is Chelsea Piers. Relatively new to the city—maybe five years old—Chelsea Piers takes up what must be the equivalent of eight city blocks bordering the Hudson River. It houses everything from photo studios to restaurants, gymnasiums, offices, bowling alleys, bars, health clubs, miniature golf, clinics . . . it's like a whole little world in and of itself. I'd been to some incredible parties there but all "on the mainland"—I'd never set sail from there, or anywhere in the state for that matter, before.

The driver helped us out and there he was, Drew, the bane of my existence as Jack and I were calling it quits. A good guy, a great guy, but trouble just the same.

"Viv-e-un." He smiled. "Great to see you."

"Hey," I said nervously. "A boat, Drew? Couldn't we just have done dinner?"

"Somehow I knew you'd say that." He grinned. He looked good. He looked different.

"So this must be the Vivian I've heard so much about?" This

came from a man who looked like he'd been sprayed from the same bottle as Sheryl. "It's great to meet you." His teeth were so white, I looked for my sunglasses. In a sharp metallic Duran-Duran-esque perfectly tailored, European for sure, narrow gray suit, he extended his hand and firmly shook mine as Sheryl and Drew and a few cats from his posse all looked on nervously.

"Hi," I said awkwardly.

"Nice to meet you. Justin. Justin Paleaze."

"Hi Justin. Great day for a sail," I said, darting a look at Drew.

"You betcha. And wait until you see this boat. Baby, it's fine!"

Mr. Paleaze was either a pill-popper or a very big boat fan.

"I'm sure I speak for all us men when I say that I hope you ladies brought your bikinis, hahaha, oops, my bad, I meant bathing suits, right guys!?!"

Collective: "Hahaha, right Justin."

Was this really happening? Sheryl chuckled, I didn't.

As we walked along the pier and then onto the boat, which wasn't a boat, by the way, but a mini yacht with a staff of twelve and every single amenity you could imagine, I firmly decided that bikini-clad I would not be. This was business and I would take it as such. I'd be polite, gracious if I could bear it, don a pretty orange life jacket, eat a free gourmet lunch, and stay within earshot of the captain. Safety first!

We checked our things with the boat's host and gave our drink orders to the bartender. I went for a mimosa (what the hell, right?) and stuck to Sheryl like white on rice. It was difficult to decide who made me more uncomfortable, Mr. Paleaze with his fake tan and fake teeth and frat-boy energy; or teddy-bear-looking Drew, who was oddly calm and confident for a guy trying to land a client in the worst economy ever; or, of course, all the hungry sharks I knew were swarming around in the waters beneath us.

The decor was flawless, an interior designer's dream. If there were a *Boat Digest* that I wasn't aware of, this little cruiser had definitely made its cover. Very *Key Largo* circa 1948. Bogart and Bacall

all the way! Retro ceiling and floor fans, palm trees and purple or-
chids in every available open space, a cigar bar, massage tables,
oversized opulent glassware, a smart collection of old books in three
bamboo-looking wall units, rich wide Hershey-brown handmade fur-
niture with plush white cotton slipcovered cushions, and, yes, two
huge flat-screen televisions and a phat sound system that even Puffy
would find satisfactory.

Talk about VIP—my oh my.

So we sat first in a cozy dining area, think fancy picnic table, at
one end of the boat and had a plethora of crudités to choose from.
One guy after the next politely excused himself to slip into something
more comfortable—after all, it was nearing ninety degrees and they
were all in suits, shirts, and ties. And one after the other they came
out with swimming trunks in awful, bright patterns pulled up as high
as their inseams would allow. (I gather it's not easy to age gracefully
as a man, either.)

Sheryl attempted to do the same, that was until I grabbed her
wrist under the table in an *I'll-kill-you-if-you-even-think-of-leaving-
me-alone* manner.

I jumped and spilled my mimosa as I heard the boat's engines
ignite, revving louder than a Harley with extra torque.

"Looks like someone's afraid of sailinnng?!?" Justin joked obnox-
iously.

"No, I'm not," I said quickly and uber-defensively. Think Sandy à
la *Grease* when Rizzo bullies her at Frenchie's sleepover to take a
"swig" from her bottle of "dessert wine."

"Are toooooo," he teased.

I looked at Drew, urging him to do something, but leave it to a
woman to step up to the plate—

"So tell us more about Supreme Vodka, Justin," Sheryl suggested. "I love your ad campaigns! What are you developing for
next season?"

As Justin babbled, I snuck away. I walked as far as I could in the
opposite direction and found a little alcove where I could collect

my thoughts. Every part of me wanted to find a life preserver worth donning for the rest of the day, but I talked myself out of it—perhaps I was letting my imagination get the best of me. A smart bench with a black-and-white thick-striped cushion, very shabby-chic-meets-cell-block-eight, made the perfect resting place. As I felt the boat begin to move, I grabbed the railing behind me with a vengeance.

Which made me laugh actually. Imagine squeezing your eyes shut, grabbing hold of something with all your might, and then waiting to blast off, take off, whatever. And then you feel the slightest of slight movements and you open one eye just a little and you can see, because the scenery begins to scroll by, and the wind is blowing through your hair and brushing against your face, that you are indeed moving but you can barely feel it. And then you feel absurd. And you laugh at yourself and slowly loosen up, and you hold, rather than grip, whatever it is that you're holding on to for dear life, and your posture reverts to normal and you begin to exhale.

It was like waiting for someone to douse me with a bucket of freezing-cold ice water and then realizing after a few seconds that I was douse-free.

That was my experience.

When I realized that I would likely live through my sailing soiree, I went crazy and actually turned around and faced the river itself. I looked left, where in the distance I could see Ellis Island and the Statue of Liberty, and when I turned my head right I had a beautiful view of the George Washington Bridge. It was all gorgeous and peaceful and very much like a postcard.

Time-outs are good, ya know? Getting a grip in the privacy of your own space—very underrated.

"You gonna jump?" I heard him say. Drew's voice over the jets of the boat's engine.

"Would you catch me?" I said.

NOT! Oh my God, I so hope you didn't think I would ever say something like that! (Sorry, just a small bit of my fifth-grade humor rearing its silly head!)

Okay, where was I? Oh, yes . . .

"That depends on how much more Mr. Paleaze has to say," I said, still not facing him, rather enjoying my view, and, sure, I was semi-flirting.

"I'm hoping to get him plastered," Drew joked. "Maybe then he'll pass out, shut up, and we can tell him how great it all went tomorrow."

"I like that plan."

"I bet you do," he said.

Silence.

"I've got some bad news . . . ," he said.

I turned to him immediately. I just knew this day would turn to crap!

"What?" I said. "Should I be sitting down?"

"Relax, Vivian. God you're wound tight these days."

I cocked my head to the side and winced at him; if he had something to say he'd best say it. And as he began, I tried, to no avail, to get the hair out of my eyes and mouth and untangled from my earrings. Charming.

"I've got to get you back there. This is business."

"I know. I know," I whined with a hint of disappointment. I'd thought and maybe hoped he'd say something "good."

eight

Fast-forward three long hours and, yes, Mr. Paleaze was out like a light. There was even a hint of drool dripping out the corner of his mouth as he sat there, almost lifeless, with his head tilted over to one side as though his shoulder were telling him a secret.

Fully wanting to stick the lone floating celery stick from his Bloody Mary up his nose and take Sheryl's black Sharpie and fashion him a cartoon Captain Hook mustache, I was foiled by Drew's suggestion that one of his minions escort their boss to the berth of the boat. ("Berth," I would come to learn, is the area in which the boat's sleeping quarters are found. I love all these new words, useless of course, but still fun to throw around.)

Soon after and much like dominoes who've had way too much to drink and taken way too much sun, one by one my sailing companions found their way to Sleepytown. Sheryl sprawled out, in full REM zone, on one of the many plush shaded sofas, using her color-coordinated sarong as a cute little blank-ee. Two of the Supreme guys, Devon and Anthony, same deal sans sarongs, lay on beach chairs at the "bow" (front) of the boat, one still miraculously balancing a glass of Chardonnay, the other basically comatose on his belly like a giant raw chicken fillet. Ronnie, the last of the Supremes, was busy playing poker with the "cruise director" guy down below.

With my coast apparently clear, I decided to finally grab Sheryl's extra bathing suit from her initialed two-toned canvas beach bag and change out of my completely soaked blouse and trousers. Hour after hour, as ridiculous as I had felt being the only one not in a swim-suit, I simply could not give Justin any viewing pleasure. The feeling of still being that awkward teenager, poolside, in a bathing suit and boxer shorts was anchored in the back of my mind, giving me a "body-conscious" label that I had proudly grown out of years— okay, a few months—ago!

With much time to go before we hit our "slip" (loading dock at the pier), I was almost looking forward to soaking up the sun, finding a private hideaway somewhere on this mansion of a boat, until I saw what Sheryl had brought for me. Enter teenie-weenie yellow (and blue and pink) polka-dot string bikini. Was she mad??? Oye.

On my way to the "head"—boat for "bathroom"—I found Drew. From what I could tell he was immersed in his *New York Times* as he sat, all too comfortably, on the boat's swim platform. Only his knees were visible, dangling worry-free in the river. With the "business" por-tion of the day already out of the way, Drew, like the rest of us, was milking this experience for all that he could. From my view, I could see his tight-ee white-ees sneaking a little peek from his black (Prada Sport—ewww) shorts-slash-bathing-suit. (Had always imagined him a "boxer" guy, hmm.) He had a bottle of Bud Light just next to him and of course, in true Drew style, a chunky black and silver aqua lasting slash looking sports wristwatch, Cartier if you must know. His "great for swim great for ski" black-and-blue iridescent sport shades were wrapped around his fleshy face, and I couldn't help but think that he'd probably picked them up in Soho, yesterday, especially for this trip.

You could tell that he had been in the water a little while before. His consciously roughed-up brown head of hair was in that in-between *I'm-almost-dry* stage, and there were still parts of his trunks sticking to his quads. The hair on his forearms was still shellacked to his tanned skin, and the delicate way he held his newspaper suggested that he had to still be careful not to get it wet.

Drew was built, not brawny, and as aware of his physicality as I apparently was. (This being one of the few questionable attributes that had kept me from pursuing him weeks and months after Jack and I were through.) His style, although great to look at, had a weirdness, too. Think "metrosexual." And honestly, all the men in my life had been clueless, taking fashion direction from me and only sometimes. None had spent obscene amounts of money on anything if it didn't have a wheel, a plug, or a door.

Then there was the whole name thing, too. Even though his business cards, his e-mail address, his voice mail, etc., read "Drew," he had admitted to me, one night after one too many shots of tequila, that yes, in fact, he had grown up as "Andrew." Now tell me, what kind of guy changes his name, officially even??? Isn't that sort of odd? Guys shouldn't care about their names, right? Unless of course they're bestowed with monikers like Ignatz or Felix. Then it's completely legit.

And then there was our timing. When we got close, as friends and as business associates, we were both in serious relationships. I had Jack and he had "Butt," my nickname for her that fit like a glove. And, honestly, I didn't really want to go down as a cheating boyfriend-stealing kinda gal, ya know.

Feeling a bit like a weirdo Peeping Tom, I *Pink-Panther*-ed it away from my vantage point and found the bathroom so I could change. My back was still a little sore, and as low as my tattoo was, this napkin of a bathing suit gave it a beachfront-property view.

So be it, I thought. The heat was unbearable.

Just about ready to go public, and then there was a knock at the door.

"One second," I screeched.

I came out, my musky clothes in a ball, and saw Ronnie, soused.

"Hey," he said, turning a quick and simple *hey* into a paragraph. Although we were arm's length apart, I could smell and almost see the alcohol floating from his breath.

"Hi," I chirped, shoving my clothes in front of me, making a shield. I crept by him and was seconds from a clean getaway until . . .

"Yo . . . nice tattoo."

"Thanks," I uttered, embarrassed as you would expect.

"Hot!" he proclaimed and I couldn't help but think of Nick and of strippers.

Oh boy.

The music went from characterless pop to soulful R&B, 'cause the shipmates knew there definitely wouldn't be anyone conscious enough to notice. I noted this and thanked them and asked for their best recommendation for premium solitary sunspace. The first mate suggested the swimming platform and when I told them that I had seen someone there a few minutes ago, he said that "Mr. Drew is having a late lunch bowside."

Very nice.

The uniformed and uber-polite first mate escorted me over to the platform, going so far as to lay down a towel for me. He asked if I wanted anything to drink and I asked for a Virgin Shirley Temple, which made him laugh a little. Another drink-ee drink, I did not need.

Sprawled out, sucking in and trying to breathe required a little effort. The sound of the water and the humming sensation of the boat and the tunes in the background made for the most perfect mood music. I brought my cell phone, Sheryl's fancy tanning oil, SPF so low it's not worth mentioning, and my *Us Weekly,* and soon had not only my refreshing cocktail but also a perfectly chilled bowl of sliced fruit. A girl could so get used to this!

Fifteen minutes passed and then I got bored. Like A.D.D. bored. So much for my inner VIP.

No one to talk to, fruit and drinks already digested, having already applied and reapplied and absolutely not even thinking about jumping in the water, and without any service (cell phone), I was at a loss.

I counted back from one hundred, visualized pretty little ballerina-costumed sheep, one after the other, prancing over my head; nada. I thought perhaps I'd check out the dessert offerings.

Back on my feet, pretending I had a bod on me like Heidi Klum and still no one in sight, I was in a piglet's splendor when I saw what I had to choose from, cake-and-pie-wise. Heaven!!!

- Pecan pie
- Apple pie
- Brownie-bottomed pie
- Crème brûlée
- Chocolate mud cake
- Chocolate mousse
- Crumb cake

Oh, yeah, and there were more of those chilled fruit bowls—whatever!

Tough choices to make for sure!

"Hell-o!" I heard behind me.

Drew.

☺

I thought that maybe if I held my breath and stood still he'd blink and then I could jet—think *Superman*—find a phone booth, change my clothes, and return at the speed of light. Forcing Drew to second-guess himself. Assume the "me" he thought he saw was a fantasy or perhaps a nightmare!

"Hi," I mumbled back. (Putting down the chocolate mud pie and okay, fine, the pecan one too!)

"How about a game of chess?" No bikini comment. No tatt comment. Drew could be a kind man.

"Chess?" I turned.

"A civilized game for civilized people," he joked. "Have you never played?"

"I have." Still distracted by the dessert.

"Then are you afraid I'll beat you?"

"No," I said. "I'm sure you'll beat me."

"So indulge me."

"All right." I followed him to the extra-large chessboard mounted on a luxe customized wooden table near the cabana just a few feet away.

So there we were. With the music and the water, the gorgeous sun, the loyal shade, the privacy and the staff, the brought-in special flowers and plants, in bathing suits, with fresh fruit and cold drinks, and I could only think of how sick this would all be if Drew was my boyfriend.

He elected to move-slash-go first and as I sat there, staring to the point of dizziness, trying to decide what to do, groping for the words of my grandfather, who'd taught me the game at least a decade ago—*the bishop does this, the queen does that . . . blah, blah blah*—Drew threw me off and sighed, "How great would this be if you and I—"

Nervous, excited, happy, scared, I could only come up with . . .

"—had money on this game?"

I looked up.

"Not exactly," he admitted.

NINE

I've never been good in social scenarios that I don't see coming a mile away. Hand me a guy whom I know-slash-think I can handle and voilà, moth to a flame. I'm so good sometimes I wish I had a third hand that could pat my back. The one-liners, the body language, the ownership of the when and where and how of the first kiss—it's genius. But throw me a curveball and ooosh, it's painful to watch. Pain-full!

Thank God for Victoria Boz and her impeccable timing!

My editrix phoned and interrupted our phony game of chess.

"Vivian, honey, bravo!" she cooed.

"Noooooooo." I wilted. Happy and astonished and fully in denial. *She couldn't really be referring to my manuscript!* A laundry list of conflicting yet moment-defining adjectives raced through my veins like a bunch of soon-to-be brides at the opening of a semi-annual Vera Wang sample sale.

"Darling, truly. You surpassed my expectations, and honey, they were high!"

"Oh, wow! I'm so glad," I blushed, excusing myself from Drew's chess game and finding an empty cushion on Sheryl's makeshift bed.

Out the corner of my eye I saw Mr. Paleaze doing a feet-to-the-floor jumping-jack-ish stretch, having just emerged from his nap, and I thought nothing of immediately, à la David Blaine at fifteen, swiping Sheryl's sarong without waking up the little cutie and making it a life-sized bib. No sooner did he walk toward me than I raised my cell phone, indicating *I'm busy,* and he, thankfully, reacted, mouthing, *Oh, okay.*

Just as I was about to continue, Mr. Paleaze came closer, this time raising his thick caterpillar of an eyebrow and pointing to Drew, wanting, I assumed, to take my place opposite him.

Instead of roaring, *What?!? You annoying rodent of a man!* I winked, happily, and tried to refocus on Victoria. But it was difficult. Mr. Paleaze was like a child with A.D.D. who didn't take his meds and thought he was entitled to proprietary rights 'cause he'd chartered a boat for the day. Our whole exchange was like one big air-kiss-and-mime job for *Yes, I'm busy* and *yes, take over for me* and *yes, don't even think about touching me unless it's our handshake good-bye!* He was just the worst, you guys. Think Rodney Dangerfield in *Caddyshack* only not funny and not Rodney.

"Where are you?" she repeated, probably for the third time, annoyed. "I've had you on my speed dial all damn day!"

"I'm sailing, a business thing, and my service blows. I'm sorry."

"Then change your service, sweetheart, I cannot not get you if I need you."

"Aye, aye," I said.

"So, I'm not going to change a thing Vivian," she informed me. "As is. As is!"

"Great."

"Stephanie is sending it to our copyeditor now. You should have it back in a few weeks for your final approval."

"I'm so relieved, V! I don't know what to say."

"Don't say anything, sweets," she said, deadpan. "Just start writing!"

"Come again?" (Writing?)

"*Book Two*, baby—it's due in six months."

"You have got to be—"

"Nope. I'm serious."

"But—"

"Got to go, V. Check your contract if you don't believe me."

"But—"

"Listen, Salomon something or other is in the lobby and I can't keep the big dogs waiting!"

"But—"

"Call you next week!"

Click.

"Victoria!!!" I whimpered. "Victoria???"

I slammed my phone shut and looked to the sky and tried to breathe. Desperately.

Who-who-he. Who-who-he. Who-who-he. Who-who-he. Who-who-he. Who-who-he.

I next visualized myself, at ninety, chained to a desk in my apartment with Victoria, who was dressed in something black and shiny and dominatrix-inspired, whipping me with Omelet's leash every time I stopped typing.

Sheryl peeped in, gaining my attention. "Are you all right, Viv? You look a little—"

I turned to Sheryl. "Is she crazy? Start writing? Writing what? My freakin' eulogy?"

Who-who-he. Who-who-he. Who-who-he. Who-who-he. Who-who-he. Who-who-he.

"Vivian, relax. You don't look very good."

Who-who-he. Who-who-he. "Another book? I'm just weaning myself off the first one, Sher." Who-who-he. Who-who-he. "I knew it was a trilogy, I just didn't realize . . ." Who-who-he. Who-who-he. Who-who-he. Who-who-he. Who-who-he. Who-who-he.

"Maybe she's mistaken, Viv?" she suggested nervously.

Who-who-he. Who-who-he. Who-who-ewwwwwwww. "Sher, I don't feel very well."

Quickly she rushed me down the hall, toward the loo, but it didn't take a genius to see that I wasn't going to make it that far. I could also feel that my left nipple was trying to figure out what all the fuss was about . . . pushing the left triangle top of my bathing suit out of the way, making sure that her Vivian was A-OK. (Yes, I was beginning to hallucinate. But my nipple was exposed at this point. Trust me.)

With Sheryl's help, and the inquiring minds of the rest of my party looking on, I had the support of many as I upchucked over the side of the boat. My nerves, coupled with the sun, the sea, and those few concocted cocktails, got to my stomach and held an uprising! Mutiny aboard—no doubt!

A little while later Drew tried to console me as I lay beside and between Sheryl and the captain, donning that life jacket, two motion-sickness bracelets on each wrist and a bright blue cold compress on my forehead on this now never-ending business trip from hell. I stared, both focusing and marveling, at my fresh pedicure in an effort to regain control of my bodily functions.

"So I guess this means you won't be joining us next week when we go bungee jumping?" he joked.

I could only remove the cold compress and come up with, "So-not-funny."

"Oh, but it is Viv, it is . . . ," he teased coyly and then, to my horror, waved his digital camera above my head in a lopsided game of "Monkey in the Middle."

"You didn't," I proclaimed, horrified.

"Or did I?" he said, then upped and walked away.

"That's just too inhuman and cruel to be believable, right?" I said to Sheryl as we both looked on and enjoyed the view. (Of Drew, BTW.)

"God, will you guys just do it already and get it over with!" she implored.

"Uh-uh," I said. "Uh-uh. The flirting is way too good, Sher."

She laughed and I continued, "Why let sex interrupt such a great working relationship?"

And as our dear captain steered us back to shore, all the while pretending not to pay us any mind, Sheryl considered my explanation and finally conceded, "Sad but true, Viv. Sad but so so true."

"They never live up to our expectations," I said.

"They don't, do they?"

"Nope," I finished. "Not when it's gone on this long."

ten

You know how you can look back at one day—sort of step out of it once it's passed—and see the huge paradigm shift in your life, so big that, for you, the planets nearly collide? Sure, things may have been in motion for months, but in your little world, the bad news, the big deals, the intercepts or introductions, it was that day that triggered everything that followed. Well, looking back and having the power now of hindsight, it's easy to see the transformation that wore me like a sweater the day after that boat trip.

It was a yucky rain-filled day, I remember, where the air felt thick and the breeze was as charming as it was reckless. The kinda day that you could swear you're seeing through your sunglasses but you're not. The kinda day that could be Halloween but isn't. The kinda day where if you could get out of going to work, ya did. The kinda day where you don't count calories 'cause you're just plain over it. It was that kind of day. Where you throw on your favorite sweats and the first clean tank top you can get your hands on. You don't shower. You venture into a designer coffee shop and buy yourself an overpriced milk shake that's disguised as something caffeine-filled and iced. You read your morning paper, spending more time in the gossip section then you do in world events. And then you find a movie that you've been wanting to see and go see it. Friendless. And you make your thick frame of mind your escort.

It wasn't even eleven A.M. and I had the best seat in the house at the Angelica, my favorite theater in all New York City. I guessed that the art-house folk didn't like their movies till after noon. With a scant few minutes before previews, I decided to use some and call Jayden and see if she still had her heart set on leaving. (Yes.)

"How are you doing, Vivian? I heard about yesterday," she said gingerly.

"Oh, I'm fine, J. No big thing. You're cool with holding down the fort till tomorrow?"

"Of course! You won't even recognize your office when you get back!"

Music to my ears . . .

"So . . . ," I began.

"Yes, Vivian. I'm still leaving," she said rather all-knowingly. "And no, it has nothing to do with you!"

"What makes you think I'd think that?" I said with a small chuckle, the only one I could find.

"You should have seen your face," she joked. "I felt like I was breaking up with you."

"Well, what can I say, ya know? Very left-field of you, J."

"I know . . . but you only live once so I figure, why not?"

God, she sounded like me. I chewed on that for a moment as she continued. "I'm going to meet with a few people today that HR suggested. I'm sure I'll find you someone great."

"All right," I said. "Knock yourself out and call me if you need me, but not for the next one hundred and five minutes."

"At the Angelica are you?"

I laughed. "Bye-bye."

Just as I hung up, my phone rang. It was Sophie.

"Hey babe!"

"Hi!"

"May said that you're not at work. You at the movies?"

"Where else." I laughed. "What's up???"

"What are you doing tonight?"

Before I could answer she said, "—because Rob and I want to take you to dinner."

"I would love that, Soph."

"Oh good!"

"Where? When?"

"I'm not sure. Let me ask Rob where he wants to go. I'll ring you back in a hundred minutes or so. 'Bye."

Loved her. And so psyched to finally meet Romeo. Long over-due.

As the lights went down and the flickering sound of the projector started in, and the delectable smell of the butter machine surrounded me like honey to bees, I instinctively darted out of my seat, ran through the exit door and into the lobby as though it were a timed obstacle course where the prize would be the most genius morning ever if I could get my Sprite on, grab a Milk Duds, and balance an extra-large bucket of salted and buttered popcorn before the featured flick began.

Insert: *The Wizard of Oz* theme music when the Wicked Witch of the West unleashes her flying monkeys . . . Da-dum da-dum da-dum dum. Da-dum da-dum da-dum dum. Da-dum da-dum da-dum dummmmmmmmmm!

As I caught my breath and fidgeted, I was relieved to spot only two people ahead of me on line and more than enough staff behind the fogged and fingerprinted glass counter to ensure a quick turnaround. I was reminded of Sophie and me, plus about fifty or so years, when I focused in on a pair of stylin' still-tryin' elderly ladies, making the most of their senior citizen pro bono time and options. Just ahead of me and with all the expected accoutrements: shiny hollow-looking black purses, matching flat foam-filled shoes, control-topped something-or-others allowing for a panty-line-less slenderized look, their trousers tailored just so. Brazen brassieres that shaped their breasts into triangles, consummately kept gray hairdos, aged, spotted hands with swollen knuckles bejeweled with tarnished platinum and diamonds, weathered gemstones, gifts and keepsakes perhaps, with a thousand stories of their own.

As they paid for their snacks, these friends, sisters maybe, moved slowly and decidedly with a stately elegance, carefully thought out and pleasant just the same. To see one help the other with her popcorn as her handbag rocked back and forth from her forearm was like watching a favorite postcard image come to life. I'd send it to Sophie for sure.

BANG!

Enter: momentary mini heart attack.

SPLAT!

Enter: Burning sensation.

What the—?

Had I been shot?

Should I "get down"?

Is everyone okay?

And, oh yeah, YOUCH!!!

I opened my eyes quickly and saw the two old ladies, with their popcorn and gummy bears and Klondike bars, straight ahead, looking at me as if I were lost as they sipped from their giant-sized candy-red slush drinks. I heard the guy behind the counter: " 'Scuse me, ma'am, I'm, ummm, real real sorry. Um, ma'am. Um. Sorry. Oh man. I'll get my manager." And then I saw him scutter off.

Still unsure what the apology was for, and my body temperature now sweltering, I put my fingertips to my face, all eight of them 'cause my thumbs didn't reach, if we're being technical (do it, you'll see what I mean), and when I put them before my eyes they looked and smelled like they had been dunked in and out of a bucket of butter for hours. I felt butter grease dripping from the tip of my nose to the tip of my upper lip. Off an eyelash, onto a cheek, and then off to my chin. I felt some slithering down my chest into my cleavage, underneath my bra and down my stomach in a perfect vertical line. And at my feet was the lid-slash-top-slash-pump contraption of that circus-looking hot butter machine that seconds before was just atop the counter.

Then it made sense even though it so didn't!

"You have got to be kidding me!!!" I said aloud. "Who gets showered by an exploding hot butter machine!!!"

"You do," one of the old women chirped in as the other nudged her with her elbow.

"Thanks, um, yes, apparently so," I said as politely and respect-fully as I could muster.

Then a Pillsbury-Doughboy-ish man of a man, pale, barely bal-ancing his thick-framed tortoiseshell glasses as he moved with a waddle not a walk, floated over with a stray piece of paper towel in his hand. Handing it to me, he said, "My apologies ma'am. My apologies. We've been having trouble with that machine all week. Please, allow me to reimburse your ticket. This morning's presenta-tion is on me."

"Reimburse my ticket?" I repeated. Was he kidding? Hey, was I on *Candid Camera*? Was I being *Punk'd*? Then maybe this would all make sense and I'd get to hang around with Ashton Kutcher! I looked around, immediately turning my shrieked-out face into an awkward contrived beauty queen smile just in case.

No cameras.

No Ashton.

No more smile.

"Okay, fine, ma'am," pushing up his glasses with his pointer fin-ger, "I'll give you a second free ticket but that is all I am authorized to do, ma'am."

Jeez—again with the *ma'ams*!

"I'm not haggling with you," I managed. "I . . . oh, just forget it. Can you point me to the nearest ladies' room please?"

He pointed and left the scene.

I swished and swashed down the hallway and into the recently bleached bathroom. I was afraid to find my reflection and getting a headache from the combined aromas. Once in front of a mirror, I truly looked like I had taken a bath in a can of Spam. Moisturized with cooking oil. Took a job on the side as a butter wrestler.

So much for my morning at the movies.

Some time later, I exited the theater in a burgundy-and-navy movie theater polyester-slash-cotton uniform complete with paper hat, with my clothes in an extra-large bucket formerly used for, yes, you guessed it, popcorn. I put my sunglasses on and sat outside on the steps of the Angelica Theater and laughed inside and then out.

This was so going in my next book.

With my hair wet from a quickie pumped-pink-soap-and-sink job, in these clothes and of course my shades, I knew that I needn't feel embarrassed because my own mother would never in a million years recognize me in my current state. So I decided to walk a bit, fearing that I had gained weight from merely absorbing what amounted to twenty sticks of butter. All too quickly I learned to step out of the way when a furry four-legged creature came a-sniffin'. Learned the hard way, I might add, after getting tongued down by a golden retriever with a fetish for spreadables.

I rounded out at Washington Square Park and very much liked being so incognito. It was now nearing noon so I thought to call May and see if she was feeling like a pretzel with or without mustard and a lukewarm Pepsi à la Mr. Vendor to my right. I told her that I'd be sitting near the chess tables closest to Sixth Avenue and she said she'd be there in "ten."

Fabulous, although I still smelled like someone had left me out when I needed to be refrigerated.

The clouds were breaking up and the sun was giving the city a little look-see as in *Maybe, just maybe, I'll come out and play.* I thought, *Fair enough.*

I eyeballed all I could while waiting. NYU students were out and about, as were the token homeless—fewer than usual, which I took as a very good sign. On the gaps of green lawns there were still the shirtless shaveless guitar-strumming nomads, the small circle of earnest students conferring over the overconferred, the ever-present *get-a-room-would-ya* couples, and I thought, *God, is time not standing still!!!* The vibe here was exactly the same as I'd left it, maybe three years before? Same backdrop, same characters . . . it (time) must get so bored.

Even the freaky skinny hairy naked guy, a fixture when I used to live in the neighborhood, clothed only in bumblebee-colored nylon short shorts, still wore makeup for some insane reason à la Lucille Ball and still carried an eighties boom box on his shoulder as he in-line skated in exaggerated figure-eights. To no music, by the way. And then there were the unemployed. Cloaked in a forced *I'm-casual-with-being-casual* dress-sort-of-down attire. Trying perhaps to be comfortable while still attempting to fool the less observant into thinking they were, instead, on lunch break. I knew better, 'cause I'd been there before. They'd only smile when they realized they weren't. They'd make a series of frustrated phone calls. They'd hop from an ambitious hardcover novel to the crinkled crackled un-kempt pages of the classified section of the *New York Times* and then back again. They'd look disturbed, then frustrated, then angry, and then almost violent as people, very employed busy people, passed them by.

Speaking of passersby . . .

"May! Hey May! May! Yo!" I called as the distance between us increased. She turned and looked around me. Perhaps I was stand-ing behind me? Perhaps I was blocking me? It was not until I took my shades off and undid my ponytail that she figured it out.

"Oh no. Oh no!" she uttered in between a few laughs and a few gasps. "I'm afraid to even ask!" she said as she plopped down be-side me—well, as much as one could plop who rocked a skintight kelly-green shrunken T-shirt, a pair of crisp just-out-of-the-dry-cleaners chino cropped pants, and the most genius black pointed patent-leather Christian Louboutin heels I'd seen all season. She looked like New York City Barbie.

"First of all," I said, "you look sick. And second, oh my God, May, do I have a story for you!"

"You'd better hope so!" she said glaring at my getup and likely catching a whiff of my new perfume.

Just as I was about to get into it, she interrupted. "Hang on Viv, hang on." She placed her newly French-manicured hands on my knee, then found my hands and squeezed them with sheer delight. As her giggles morphed into cackles and my "costume" began to itch she confided, "I can't take it anymore. You've got to hang on one sec because, Vivian, honestly, I have got a story for you!"

Enter: shots of thunder and lightning.

eleven

I sat there transfixed as May began to divulge, both of us oblivious to Mother Nature's warning signs.

"I don't know how to tell you this . . . ," she began, and I swear to you that if she hadn't been smiling I would have thought she was eloping with Jack. Because you and I both know that when someone close to you tells you that she doesn't know how to tell you something, it's almost always horrifyingly bad. "But, I've been sort of 'involved' with someone and we agreed that we wouldn't say anything to anyone, but he just surprised me with this . . ." She pulled a tiny tiny gray-and-white blue-eyed kitten from her cherry-red-jelly Hermès-ish bag.

"Oh my . . . ," I said, inching away from the both of them. (I'm deathly afraid of cats. Long story and so not important in the scheme of things.)

"Awwww, V. Don't be afraid," she purred as she held the little thing up in the air the way fathers do their babies. "Smitten is just the most delicious little kitten."

"Smitten?" I laughed.

"Yup. Our Smitten little kitten," she said as google-ee as you might expect.

I started to chuckle, not exactly laugh, in a self-pitying way. I just couldn't help it. Apparently while I was hidden away writing my novel, everyone around me had been bitten by a love bug.

A lone tear, the kind that emerges due to happiness, peeked from her left eye. "Oh my God, V, I never . . . I never thought I could be this happy, ya know?"

"Yeah, I know," I said, irritated, not by May but by the material of my uniform. She was oblivious. She placed Smitten in her lap and waited for my next expected question . . .

"Does Smitten's daddy have a name?" I asked.

"Yup," she said coyly, petting Smitten.

"Well, are you going to tell me?"

"It's [laughs] it's [more laughs] . . . Daniel!" Giggling and then hiding her face in her hands. "It's Daniel! Can you even believe it!"

"Oh my God. YES. I can so believe . . ." (I'd be lying if I hadn't imagined myself with him on a few separate occasions!)

"I know—crazy, right?"

"No, May, it's the most sane thing I've ever heard. He's a man-sandwich! Oh my. And that accent!"

"You have no idea, V. He's . . . the best."

"The best?"

"The best."

I shook my head in utter envy. (The good kind.) Daniel, Drew's assistant, was, as I've said before, one of the hottest guys I've ever seen in real life. And according to May, he was the sweetest and most thoughtful guy in the world.

"He just makes me feel so, so, so . . . beautiful."

"You are!"

"He thinks I'm smart—"

"You are!"

"Aw, thanks, V. But you know how much different it is when a guy makes you feel that way. I mean, I always thought I felt good about myself, ya know, but he, Daniel, well, he just solidifies every-thing. And not because I need a man to do that, it's just, well, it's just such an affirmation. I think that's how the right guy is supposed to make you feel."

English was beginning to feel like a second language. I didn't know what she meant . . . I didn't know what she meant, I didn't know what Sophie meant, and I didn't know what Sheryl meant. I couldn't understand why Jayden would up and leave, why Marni would get married so young. What was wrong with me!!! I hid my sudden panic attack as best I could and used facial expressions instead of words as a signal for May to continue, 'cause I knew for sure that if I spoke I'd get choked up.

"We were working late, remember, the night we were working on the redesign of the Web site?"

"Yeah . . ." I did. Sort of.

"And we were the last to leave. And when we left the office and were waiting to catch a cab we realized that we lived only blocks from each other."

"Yeah . . ."

"And so we shared a cab and got out right by that relatively new dim sum place—"

"The one we took Sophie to for her birthday?"

"Yup. And he asked if I wanted to grab a bite to eat with him. And I said sure and didn't think anything of it. And then when we asked for a table for two the hostess said that the wait would be over an hour and in the same breath suggested we get something to go. So we did, separate bags and everything, and just as I was about to say good night he asked if I wanted to come up to his place and we could eat there."

"All right," I said. It all sounded good so far.

"So, I get up to his apartment. And it makes mine look enor-mous. It's one small room with a bathroom—that's it."

"Oh, I remember those days," I said nostalgically.

"I know. So he said that the place had one redeeming quality, and I asked what that was, and he told me to follow him and he grabbed my hand and escorted me to his roof deck. I still didn't really think much of it. You know, that anything was going to happen. Anyway, it was gorg! With a small table and a few tiki torches and you could see the entire Flatiron District and it was magnificent."

"So . . . ," I said impatiently. All these details were great but I was dying for "the part"!

"Okay, sorry," she apologized. "So he runs back down and comes back with a bottle of white wine and a book of matches. He lights the torch thing-ees and we just have the most amazing dinner. He tells me all about London and his family and I talk about film school and Stan and you and my sister and before I realize it, it's almost midnight and we've finished our second bottle of wine."

"You're killing me, May! Spill!!!"

"All right, all right!" she said. Laughing, stroking Smitten, suffering from lovestruck attention deficit disorder. "And he tells me that I have a wonderful smile."

"He does not!"

"He does! And I blush and say thank you. And I want to tell him that he has wonderful everything but I can't and as I'm speechless, he leans across the table and just kisses me!"

"No, no he does not!"

"He does! And V, honest, I have never been kissed like that. Like ever!"

"And then . . . ," I ask, dying for the details.

"Well, let's just say we woke up on the roof deck at about six A.M.!"

"You're so bad!" I teased.

"I know!" she squealed. "And, well, it's been so amazing ever since. It's crazy. Every morning I wake up expecting him to lose interest, dump me, upset me, and, well, nothing! It just gets better and better."

"I bet," I said, looking at Smitten.

"Ahhhhhh," she said, breathing a sigh of relief. "I feel so much better now. Holding it in all these months."

"Months?" I was shocked.

"Yup. About three. Three months and two and a half weeks to be exact."

"I can't believe you didn't tell me!" I said, my mind utterly blown. And seriously, if she had given me that "trimester" babble I would have needed to disown her.

"I couldn't. I barely saw you and when I did we were always with a bunch of other people and besides, I was afraid."

"Afraid?"

"Not of you, no. I was afraid that it wouldn't last. I didn't want anyone to know, not because of the whole work thing, that's his reasoning, just because, well, he's so unbelievable that I was afraid he'd let me down. I just wanted to be sure that it was real before . . . and besides, having a "work thing" is so scandalous! In the best way of course! It's fun when you know that no one else knows. It's like a private little world that you share."

"I can only imagine," I said, thinking, for a moment, of Drew.

She made me promise not to tell a single soul and not to let on to Daniel that I knew. I promised. She asked me to pet Smitten and I did with the tip of my pointer finger . . . on his back. Then she asked me to go home and change before we both saw someone we knew, and I agreed.

"What are you doing tonight?" she asked as she scooped up Smitten and dusted off her tush.

"I'm going to meet Sophie and Rob. Dinner. Something like that," I said, still seated with a bucket of clothes at my feet.

"Oh, you'll love him. He's the best," she said. Still, I couldn't help but think that anyone and anything would be "the best" in May's current condition. "What do you think of my outfit?" I said.

To myself, it turned out: She was on her merry way before you could say *Perfect* and I remained seated listening to another shot of thunder and lightning à la Ms. Nature.

My phone started to ring and I flipped it open with a "hello" flat as unleavened bread.

"Hey." It was May. "I feel so bad. You didn't even tell me your story!"

"Oh, it's nothing. No worries."

"You'll fill me in tomorrow?"

"Of course," I said.

"Love you, V."

"You too, babe."

It started to rain and I didn't care. If anything it might rinse the stink off me. Despite my previous mood, my personal pep talks, the whole lot of it, I couldn't help but feel congenitally defective. Up and down, up and down, day in and day out. My mood was bouncing around like the dots above sentences that instruct us to sing along. Exhausting, I tell ya! Again I worried: Had Jack been on to something? I mean, his last tirade had all been about my inability to trust and to love. At the time I couldn't help but think that it was *him* I had the problem with. Nothing inbred, ya know? But with love all around me and not a single prospect in sight, maybe he was right? And that morning after, after the proposal and after my no, my parents and their furiousness. My mother barking her disappointment and contempt: "How many times will a great man want you?" It went something like that. Maybe she was right.

Cell phone again . . .

"Hello," I mumbled.

"Vivi?" It was Sophie. "Is everything okay?"

"Yeah, of course. What's up?"

"Dinner—eight o'clock—Cipriani's?"

"You got it," I said, borrowing some chipper from the few birds searching for bread crumbs at my feet.

"Can't wait!" she teeheed and hung up.

Yeah, me either.

twelve

Try as I might to get out, I was now firmly stuck in a rut and only hours away from subjecting myself to even more *I'm-so-in-love-ness*. Uch. Like sour milk . . .

Now, now, don't go judging me. Put yourself in my situation if it hasn't happened to you already—okay, I'll be nice and a little less bitter: If it hasn't happened to you *before* . . .

Moving on, I decided that a bodacious bubble bath was in order. I had time enough and I felt deserving and I was way in the mood and in need o' many bubbles. I searched for the perfect candle with just the right scent to burn. (Almost as many around my apartment as the Cosabella underwear I told you about.) Something vanilla-ee, I thought. Aren't candles the greatest and most harmless luxury purchase? They put you back twenty-some dollars but look superchic and, in the right environment and on the right occasion, create an ambience in a split second! So, me love my wax! (Fresh and Swoon Candles are my very faves . . . but I digress.)

I turned the water on, flipped over my bubble bath serum, and squeezed the bottle dry. Not wanting to leave Omelet out, I indulged him, too, with a fistful of his very favorite gourmet peanut butter treats and then scrambled through station after station for some mood-appropriate light FM on my already ancient stereo. Finally I switched the lights off, got naked, and ahhhhhhhhhhhhh.

With the soft serene semisilence that occupied my newly created home spa, it was difficult to clear my head at first. I thought about business, about the books, about my bills . . . and the freaking DJ was babbling, albeit in a whisper, but he was going on and on and on. I got fidgety and turned, feeling the warm water glide over the dip in my neck, the area just where it becomes my back, and couldn't help but poke toe after wrinkled toe into the spout (is that the right word or is it faucet?). Why I—and I'm sure we all—do that is seriously a mystery to me. Anyway, I continued, enjoyed the sensations as the thousands of bubbles ravished every inch of my skin, and it was then that I started to get into it. Relaxed enough to stop counting the lone hairs that were stuck to the walls of my shower. To not concern myself with my movements, no longer afraid that a bubble or two would fall overboard. I watched Omelet, sprawled out over the checkered tiled floor, as he raised his head, moving it ever so slightly, trying to trace and then follow the scent of my candle I guessed. He couldn't have looked any more edible. Like a shrunken polar bear with an affinity for the simpler and the finer things of life. We shared a glance and, well, it was as good as if not better than swallowing a Vicodin.

My imagination along with my memory soon meandered toward Jack . . .

To a time when we both had been receiving buckets of guilt from our families whenever we individually broached the topic of staying with the other for Thanksgiving and not spending it at home. See, we were in our sixth week, and the idea of a long weekend away from one another had Romeo-and-Juliet-ness written all over it. Unable to not offend nor wanting to play favorites, we decided to take a little lovers' weekend somewhere and pay homage to the holiday in our own way! Twenty minutes later we were on the Internet and with a click of a button a trip for two to Paris (yes, France, not Texas) was booked! He used his frequent flier miles and I redeemed a free ticket I got after getting bumped off a flight home from a tech convention in San Francisco some months before. It was spontaneous and wild and sooooo romantic!

Paris?!? I simply couldn't believe my own ears when I gave my mom my reason for not being able to make her turkey fest. However, in true Vivian-esque style, nothing is ever simple or easy or ever goes exactly as planned!

Long story short, our trip there was a nightmare. From delayed flights and horrendous weather conditions to a lost (temporarily) piece of luggage and then a swank hotel that confused the word *deal* with *steal*. Our room rate was five times what had been advertised. Both of us exhausted, neither knowing a single French word other than "fries" and "toast," it was obvious that we weren't ready to fight the good fight with the snooty Parisian concierge, so we agreed to stay there for the first night and then find somewhere a little less ridiculous come sunrise. So much for the most romantic city in the world . . . or so I thought.

Exhausted from our journey, the first thing we did was sleep. The local time had to be about six P.M. or so, and the plan was that we would power-nap it till eight, shower, and then have our first fabulous French dinner at nine thirty. Good plan.

Well, it could have been. If the front desk had ever made the wake-up call we ordered. I remember going from the most heavenly sleep to some horrific nightmare when I woke up, in a near panic, knowing that it was well past eight. I quickly looked at the clock beside our bed, nearly throwing out my neck in the process, and when it said one forty-five A.M. I was stuck, frozen, somewhere between furious and disappointed. Until . . .

Well, until I saw Jack. He was at the door in the middle of removing his coat, and when he saw that I was just about to go on a tirade, with the phone in my hand, he climbed onto the bed, grabbed the phone from my hand, put it back on the receiver, and kissed my forehead. His cold cheeks and freezing nose brightened up my sheet-bruised face. "Shhhhhhhh," he whispered and lifted me out of my bed. Once he managed to get my weight and his weight shifted just so, he carried me into the bathroom. There he had a bubble bath waiting for me—my first bubble bath since kindergarten probably—and I was overcome. Never had I been surprised by a man, in the right way. Never had anyone been so thoughtful. He was so calm, so easygoing. He was my opposite in so many ways, which made us great together. I felt giddy and embarrassed and awkward and excited all at once and he could see that. He switched off the lights, leaving only the hall one on, and began undressing me slowly.

I remember trying so hard to relax, to play it cool and play it sexy. But I couldn't. I shivered every time I felt the touch of his hands. I got ticklish all of a sudden in places I had never been ticklish before. And the few times I tried to say something, lighten the mood, he just "shhhhh'd" me. I simply was not prepared to feel that good. Like ever. And so did not know how to deal.

He asked me to get in the tub, which I did and then, immediately, without his okay, I held my breath and hid under the water. I smiled the largest smile my face had ever seen and felt the happiness that I was barely blocking while Lance Romance up there was trying to seduce me. I felt so lucky and I knew that I loved him. When I giggled some water unexpectedly shot up my nose and it was by then—twenty seconds later—high time I resurfaced.

Forever aquatically challenged.

By the time I wiped the water from my eyes and disengaged my held nose, there was Jack, still in his jeans and his sneakers and his sweater, but on his knees, leaning over the tub, right there, almost waiting for me. His elbows rested atop the porcelain. His sweater was decorated already with bubbles here and there. He smiled right through me.

He was, simply, the light in my life.

He had this incredible capacity to make me feel like a giddy little girl and a fabulous frisky fraulein all at the same time.

As serious as we both tried to be, it wasn't long before we were laughing wildly. It was so cute, I remember. As he started undressing, trying to maintain eye contact with me, the buckle of his undone belt got stuck in the toe of his oatmeal wool socks as he climbed out of his jeans. He nearly toppled over, looking as if he were playing a one-man version of a potato-sack race.

Ugh. I had to stop there. This was torture. I stood up, turned the knob from bath to shower, and ordered cold water in a hurry. I rinsed off, flicked my light switch on, and blew that candle out. Did he have to forever ruin baths for me, too! What good are great memories??? I vote that they all be exfoliated and washed away if we happen to come across one in a "bittersweet" file clogged off in our hearts. All in favor say Aye!

I was in major need of a new frame of mind. I searched my record collection, which I'd alphabetized on a pathetic and lonely Saturday night some months before, and thought the Beastie Boys would do the trick, "Paul Revere" style. Drastic times, drastic measures. I fed Omelet and, thankfully, rescued the tie to my cotton bathrobe before it got inadvertently flushed down my toilet. And then my phone rang:

"Hey baby!" Sophie proclaimed excitedly.

"Hell-ooooooooooo," I faked enthusiastically.

"Change of plans," she informed me. "We're going to go to Jean George instead." Easily one of Manhattan's best French restaurants.

"But you hate French food," I said, confused.

"I know . . . ," she sighed playfully. "But Rob loooooves it and its his favorite place so . . ."

"Is it his birthday?" I mumbled.

"Huh?" Sophie said. "I didn't hear you."

"I said . . . have it your way. Wherever is cool. Same time?"

"Naaaah. We're thinking about ten now. There's some game he doesn't want to miss . . . You know how guys are."

"Oh, I so do," I quipped.

"Okay babe-ee, we'll see you a little lay-ter! Can't w-a-i-t!"

"Me n-e-i-t-h-e-rrr."

Click.

I fought off a split-second attitude like a hypochondriac does contact in a crowded emergency room. *Don't read into it,* I thought. *Don't read into it.*

With my schedule now wide open and even more time to sit around and mope, I knew better than to spend it at home while Jack was still lurking about. I suited up, grabbed Omelet's leash, and decided to take an early-evening stroll. Strolls are a godsend if your timing is right. What's better than a beautiful evening walking against a light wind in cushy comfy clothes with your treasured pet by your side?

Block after block, I people-watched, played my own game of grown-up hopscotch—don't step on the lines that divide the pavement—and periodically watched the sun in its mysterious setting mode. I was thrilled to notice someone noticing me (hey, every little bit helps)—a guy checking me out on the opposite side of the street—and although he was with his wife and child, I still let it count. (He mad me feel pretty and I couldn't remember the last time I had.) And then, an epiphany: I realized that there was a strong chance I was alone because I hadn't been "out there" for almost a year. What? I mean, is some guy supposed to get a premonition that some hot little mama, *moi,* is ready and available hidden miles and miles away behind layers and layers of cement and bricks? My prospects while in book mode were few and far between. And believe me, had any of the delivery boys been cute, I would've jumped on the opportunity! I just needed to get out more and now was my chance! It all sounded right, in theory anyway. But theory didn't wipe away the second and third and fourteenth thoughts I had about Jack.

As we reached the dog run, I let Omelet free, technically. (The park being properly fenced, I hardly think *free* is appropriate, but I digress . . .) Anyway, soon after, I thought back to Carolyn. She'd been a mentor to me when I'd first started working at VH1. Older and, I assumed, wiser—maybe not. It was way before I had even met Jack, back in my (very) early twenties and after another one of my *I-should-have-seen-it-coming* relationship debacles. Besides feeling like my job was at a dead end, that the city would forever be too big, too mean, and too foreign, when I was piss broke and suffocated by feelings of inadequacy she sat me down and assured me that our twenties are always a nightmare and that once we hit thirty things get so much better. "We know who we are, what we want," she told me. "We've grown out of pining for the silly meaningless stuff and we finally wake up and make a mad dash for what counts. We hit our stride. You'll see." Hmmmm.

Maybe I shouldn't have put so much stock in her advice. Thirty was fast approaching and not that much had changed. I wished that I could I simply twitch my nose à la Barbara Eden as Jeannie in, of course, *I Dream of Jeannie,* and get there already! Would I then find love, have my career in order, oh, and would I have a great apartment??? (Sorry, just asking!)

My twenties were wearing me down. Everything was so dramatic. Either really great or really bad. And I was exhausted. So stuck in the present that I couldn't visualize my future. And instead of busting my ass trying to locate the glimmer in this particular scenario, I decided to accept my depression rather than dwell on it. So there! I was trying too hard to find the silver lining. I mean c'mon: One guy (utterly creepy on the opposite side of the street) acknowledges my presence and all of a sudden "I'm back"? Fueled and ready to get back out there? I don't think so!

I had spent so many years as my own motivational speaker that honestly, if some studio head, TV producer, or the like with ESP had run into me, I would have had my own one-woman cable-access early-morning inspirational program in no time. Do you believe? Hallelujah! All that good stuff.

But a positive attitude gets old and it gets tiring. And I know; they're essential and priceless in this lifetime BUT mine was so exhausted! I felt the need for a boyfriend of my own. Shocking, I know—this from the fearless female who had just thrown a perfectly good one back in the sea. (Clarity doesn't always come on time, ya know.)

It wasn't that I NEEDED a man, I WANTED one. More than a girlfriend, a doggy, I wanted to find my partner. Someone who cared about me as much as he cared about himself. Someone to cheer me on. Someone to watch TV with!!!

Sniff. Sniff.

Hang on . . . where's Omelet? Oh yes, there he is. Hamming it up among several adorable cocker spaniels. How is it that even my dog gets more play than I do?

Utterly depressing.

I was craving intimacy, is all. Emotional intimacy. It had been ages—if it had even ever existed before. I had done what I'd set out to do: move to the city, find the right job, get over my past, get in touch with the real me. The me that is the woman I am, or rather, that I became. Independent, gutsy, hardworking, creative, admit my visions and follow them. Done! Did it!

Now what?

What are accomplishments, big and small, if you don't have someone to share them with? My friends, as anyone's would, were all realizing their own. Being on my own wasn't as satisfying as I had always thought it would be.

Bottom line—I wanted love.

It's funny when realizations hit you. I had a major to-do list all checked off but one. And without the balance of intimacy, again, I arrived at the same conclusion: The rest of it couldn't hold a candle.

Great!

This was about the time that I noticed that I was part of an overwhelming majority at the dog run. Single women. *Time to go!* I panicked. I was the total package—cliché-wise.

I rushed Omelet out and caught the first cab back to my apartment. So much for my stroll.

I was hanging on by a very thin thread. A yo-yo. Up, down, positive, negative. And this was before I had the distinct pleasure of meeting Rob.

thirteen

I got to Jean George early and found a seat at the bar. A cocktail felt like a prerequisite, and you know what a good student I am!

I'd decided to dress up for the occasion. I mean, how many times do you get a chance to make a first impression on the guy you think your best friend is going to marry? And I desperately wanted to make a good impression. I had this great chino Katayone Adeli suit from a Barneys warehouse sale that I treasured. No matter how many seasons would go by or what length or fit would come in and out, this little suit had stood the test of time. Shrunken blazer, with a cute enlarged heart-shaped wooden button, flat-front slightly bell-bottomed trousers, and Sophie's macramé-ish gold cami under-neath. I rocked my shiny satin olive sling-backs and grabbed a black patent rectangular clutch bag to go with. I felt like the fourth Char-lie's Angel. I let my hair dry as it rested ever so neatly in the knot I tied it in and donned a pair of gold dangly earrings that Sheryl had given me for Christmas last year. Finally there was the matter of my lipstick, my one never-leave-home-without product. I went for a wine red I'd gotten for free in a gift with a purchased makeup case at a Nars counter just the week before.

Bottom line: I had made the effort and as a result, I felt pretty damn good.

I sat at the bar, alone, in what amounted to a sea of married suited-up men. All middle-aged, stalling likely, none too desperate to get home. I don't want to assume, but that's the vibe I was getting. Afraid to make eye contact with any of them, I chose to familiarize myself with the fine top-shelf selection of Jean George's bar. But before I could even begin, I heard, "Vivian?" coming from beside me. And there was Gina, Jack's sister, whom I hadn't seen since D-day—i.e., the night of the failed proposal. Ugh.

"Hey," I said hesitantly.

"You're looking well," she half sneered, half smiled.

"And so are you—who!" I gasped, noticing her enlarged belly. "Oh my gosh, Gina, when are you due?"

"What!" she yelled, almost foaming at the mouth. "You think I'm . . . that I'm . . . the nerve of you!"

Okay. Somebody shoot me. "I—I—ayayi!" I couldn't find words. And I leaned back as far as I could in my seat, trying to put as much space between my face and her fist as possible.

"What's goin' on, G?" another voice, a southern-accented voice, chimed in. Afraid to look away, in absolute fear of being blind-sided, I caught a quick glimpse of a girl. A very very pretty girl.

"This . . . ," Gina almost explained, but then paused and took a moment, looking me and then "her" up and down. "Oh, nothing," she continued, her voice changing swiftly to an uber-sweet-and-sour sarcasm that only a fool would not pick up on. "Honey," she said, addressing the unidentified woman, "this is Vivian, and Vivian"—she turned and addressed me—"have you met Grace, Jack's GIRLFRIEND."

Okay, gloves off.

"Hiya," she peeped, extending her fragile hand and perfectly polished red nails toward me. "Niiiiice to meet cha."

I had no words. I looked at Gina, whose grin was menacing, and I just plain refused to give her the satisfaction.

"Hi there!" I smiled, so big I nearly tore skin where my dimples would have been had I inherited them from my father. "It's soooo great to meet you."

"Well, thanks!" she cooed, flipping her locks to and fro, exposing her near-perfect jawline and Sophie-esque button nose.

"Vivi! Vivian!" A shout registered from the entryway. I looked past Gina and Grace and there was Sophie, in a summertime golden poncho with a shiny white tank top peering out from underneath. Her hair in a last-minute pony, I remember, clutching a periwinkle Tod's bag, she looked like a Californian fashionista. Rob, I gathered, stood behind her, with a lone hand placed on her shoulder. Tanned, handsome in a neo-preppy sort of way, bearing a forced lip-locked grin. Oye. "Hey baby!" she smiled, coming toward me.

"Hi honey!" I said nearly shoving Gina as I broke through the two of them and hugged Sophie almost to death.

"Help," I whispered in Sophie's ear. I pulled away from her and looked her in the eye, signaling *trouble* with a capital *T*.

Sophie looked on and greeted Gina cautiously as I told Rob it was nice to meet him sans any focus whatsoever. Before he could even respond I stepped back into the circle of death, grabbed Sophie's hand, and introduced her to Grace.

"Soph," I said, "have you met Grace, Jack's GIRLFRIEND?" clenching her hand so hard I could feel bone.

"Wow." PAUSE. "No," she said looking at me with masked pity. "Nice to meet you."

Rob, my new favorite person, for real, interrupted to let us know that our table was ready. I disappeared without any social graces and gave the hostess my drink order before we'd even gotten to our seats.

Minutes later, as Rob was giving me the standard *I've-heard-so-much-about-you blah, blah, blah*, Sophie grabbed his hand and said, "Honey, hang on. That was, well, Viv, you explain."

I did the best I could, trying hard to not be "that friend," the one who's single and a mess and requires emotional first aid at every social call, even though I so was. And he laughed in a chuckling sort of way. And replied, "Wow, Vivi, jeez, I'd be freaked out, too. Is that girl a Victoria's Secret model?"

And it was there that I knew that I was in trouble.

First, the less obvious: *Vivi* was a nickname that only three people ever called me . . . my mother and Sophie and Mark. So, what was that about?

And second, well, I'm sure I don't have to spell that one out.

"Rooooob," Sophie whined, seminervously.

"What?" he said rather nondefensively. "You'd have to be blind not to see that she's—"

"Rob!" she barked and with that he shut his mouth, practically permanently.

The rest of the night, which lasted a cool forty-five minutes, was everything you might assume. While Rob placed bets with his bookie on his cell phone, Sophie tried to convince me that Grace didn't hold a candle, that Gina did look pregnant and anyone, or at least almost anyone, would have made the same assumption about her current state.

"How beautiful is my baby?" he interjected, and I looked for the wallet photo I assumed he'd break out, never knowing that he was a divorcé with a child.

"Come again?"

"My Sophie," he announced. "Is she not a vision?"

I looked at him apologetically and then to her. She was beaming. "She is . . . a vision," I agreed. And she was.

"Baby," he purred, "I'm beat and I have a full day of golf tomorrow."

"But," she stumbled, not wanting to offend me nor bail while I was in crisis.

"Honey, it's fine. Really. I'm tired anyway," I said as Rob, credit card in hand, signaled for the check.

"Are you sure?" she asked as Rob stopped a busboy who had a full tray of dirty dishes in his hands.

"Hey," he said. "Give this to our waitress, will ya?" And flopped it atop an empty salad plate.

"Baby, sign the thing-ee for me, all right? I see Alex—"

"Alex?" she questioned.

"Alex, baby, from the beach," he said while getting up, placing his wrinkled used-up napkin on the table and over my cell phone, by the way. "Vivi it was great meeting you. Great. We'll do this again."

"Sure," I said.

"Baby, if I'm not at the bar I'll catch us a cab . . . outside."

"Oh, okay," she said. With that he vanished.

I smiled, the kind of smile that makes you look constipated, not wanting Sophie to think anything but happy thoughts. Before too long our bill came, she did her thing, and she was out.

"I'll call you tomorrow," she said. "Isn't he—"

"Adorable." I smiled. "He's great, Soph."

"I know it!" she peeped and gave me a kiss and a hug and disappeared.

That was the moment our friendship changed forever.

As I waited patiently for a vacant cab, I tried not to think about Grace. Which was, honestly, a Jedi mind trick that even Yoda would find miraculous. Instead I thought about the movie *My Best Friend's Wedding*. When Julia Roberts (Julianne) watches Dermot Mulroney (Michael) and Cameron Diaz (Kimberly) leave for their honeymoon and realizes that he (Dermot) didn't even say good-bye. But then he does. He comes back and there's that second when their relationship is validated and although things were going to be different from there on out, still something would forever be the same. Do you remember? Well, I was stuck with Julia's first feeling. It had been more than fifteen minutes and Sophie hadn't reappeared.

I was inches from tears. Between Sophie and Grace and Gina, I felt sick. Still waiting, alone, in the street, watching couples pass me, holding hands and making out, and miniature groups of friends laughing it up, sharing one story or another, I was miserable.

I searched through my bag and found enough change to hop on the next bus I saw. Which was another bad move. I mean, what's more depressing then a vacant bus, just you and three other people, seated in emptied corners, exhausted, on their way home likely after a hard day's work where even payday is a constant letdown? Making matters worse, the lights were on, full blown, as if an interrogation were impending.

I caught my reflection in the window, and I didn't know who I was anymore or how I'd landed in the place I was, both emotionally and physically. What was happening? My life was spinning out of control in a cruel slow-motion kind of way, and I felt as though I couldn't do a thing about it. Making matters worse, a smelly homeless-looking guy opted to move his seat and sit next to me for no apparent reason. I debated over what was worse, offending him and getting up or offending him and asking him to move.

Before I could make up my mind, the bus stopped, yet again. That's what bites about buses: They stop on every single solitary street corner, making what should be a fifteen-minute ride an hour-and-fifteen-minute one. And who steps onto the bus, you'll never guess, so I'm just going to have to tell you. Ready: Nick. Ink boy Nick. Gorgeous-vision-out-of-a-heavy-metal-music-video Nick. The tattoo artist.

I was too distracted by Pepé Le Pew to consider the evidence and factor in whether or not seeing him made me feel good or bad and before I could decide if I wanted to make my presence known, he saw me as he walked by trying to figure out where he felt like sitting. (Odds are it was probably miles away from "us.")

"Heeeeey," he said hoarsely. "I know you."

"Uh-huh," I said.

"You're the rose-girl . . . Vivian, right?"

I was so happy that he remembered my name.

He looked puzzled, trying to figure out how and why I was sitting with this man on a very empty extra-long bus.

"Have you met my boyfriend . . . ?" I joked, and with that he gestured for me to get up and sit with him. I happily obliged, rising from my seat. I grabbed his hand and awkwardly maneuvered myself out of the small space as if I were caught inside four freshly painted wet walls.

"Happy to see me I bet," he said.

"You have no idea." I patted his thigh three times in a harmless thank-you gesture.

We spent the next half hour catching up. Small talk, for sure, but I enjoyed it and I got the vibe that he did, too. He looked great and smelled kinda good in that after-hours, few-beers kinda way. He was wearing a hooded old hunter-green logoed sweatshirt with a striped blue-and-white collared shirt underneath and a pair of deep blue denim baggy jeans. An older version of Justin Timberlake post-'NSync. His sneakers were new, very new, Pumas I think, maybe Converse, I don't remember. Needless to say, it was all working. Oh and yes, the tattooed knuckles were still there, but I did my best to pretend they weren't. When we realized that we were getting off at the same stop, he asked me if I wanted to go for a drink. I didn't have to think twice and said yes immediately.

We exited the bus, and before we even turned the corner, he grabbed my hand.

Oh. Okay, I thought, and instead of overthinking it, I went along for the ride. And, oh, girls, I should probably tell you now, what a ride it turned out to be!

fourteen

I woke up the next morning with a strange skinny pale guy sprawled out on my bed. And I'm still not too sure if it was his snoring or the lone mole on his ass that finally did him in. With the backdrop of NYC, the tattoo parlor, or a dark dingy bar, "this" made some sort of sense but without it, amid my pretty pink bedding, with the sunlight pouring through the gaps in my sherbet-colored shades and Omelet and I, both backed into the corner, standing upright, I wearing only a light blue blanket and Omelet with a stinky chewed-up piece of month-old rawhide in his mouth, we, transfixed, wondered what the deal was with the strange alien among us, all the while so knowing that "this" was one monumental step backward for womankind everywhere and a giant moment in my history that I so wished I could delete.

Why we think that a few hours of musky unfamiliar sex is going to make all the pain go away is still a mystery to me. I couldn't help but wish that I could leave and avoid what was coming entirely, but being that we'd shacked up at my place I was trapped. Terrific.

I had always prided myself on my "record." Last night, this very morning, was a first for me. (And I'm not just saying that because my mom reads my novels—promise.) I had always been too neurotic, and oddly enough too arrogant, to let a guy have me just like that. I required effort. (Let's be honest: not all that much effort. But effort just the same.) What could I have been thinking???

With that my stinkin' alarm clock went off, and before I could hide behind my curtains, knuckle boy turned over, gave me a view that haunts me to this day, and whispered, "Hey darlin'."

☺

"Hi," I said, and waved awkwardly with one hand, nearly losing my blanket in the process.

As Nick went to get up, Omelet moved in, staring at him, sitting just inches from him growling into his rawhide.

"Friendly?" he asked nervously.

"Sometimes." I giggled.

"All right then," he responded patiently. "It's cool. Hey. You wanna get that?"

"Huh?"

"The alarm clock."

"Oh, yeah, sorry."

"You're a little freaked out," he questioned as I moved gingerly across the room. My blank-ee, trailing, following suit.

"No, no, I'm fine. Fiiiiine," I urged, petrified and still hiding behind whatever fabric I had left.

"Come here." He gestured me to get back into bed.

And again Omelet with the growl.

"I'm going to take him for a walk. He's, well, he's a little protective."

"I don't blame him."

"Yeah." I laughed while combing my room for anything decent to escape in. Before too long I suited up in something Juicy-related and told him to not wait around; that Omelet's walks were more an event than a task and that I'd give him a call.

I don't remember what he said at that point, if anything at all. I just remember using every bit of strength I had to pull Omelet from my room and get him out the door. As I walked to the dog run, I could swear that the dads and old ladies who passed me were giving me dirty looks. I couldn't think of any positives that I could attribute to the experience. I couldn't remember if it was good or not, I was pissed 'cause I had just done a laundry, comforter and all, and I knew that that was a number one on my to-do list the minute I set foot back at home. I could only think of Grace, that cellulite-free mega-babe who was probably nicer and kinder than any stuffed plush bear. How happy she must be making Jack. I pictured them at Bubby's in Tribeca having brunch at that very moment. She probably ordered the French toast and he was definitely craving his eggs Benedict, all over Bloody Marys for two!

Ew!!!

At the dog run, I sat at the bench I often do, this time no paper, no coffee, and only a sliver of self-respect left. I watched Omelet greet his fans, and for a moment I hoped he wasn't blabbing. (I also hoped Nick didn't make off with my new DVD player.) When a sweet beige poodle looked over at me and then, just as quickly, looked away, I got a little insecure. Still, on the bright side, I knew that there was one plus: The beauty of one-nighters in your womanhood is that no one ever has to know. (Unless you write a nationally published tell-all, of course.) There's no walk of shame, no roommates—thank God.

A little while passed and I sat there, solemnly, picking the polish off my nails, feeling the sun flash against my forehead, and thinking back to the (late) night before. We went to Maggie's, I remembered, a dive bar in Nolita that I've been to, mostly after hours, maybe three or four times. It was just the two of us and the mysterious space, i.e. sexual tension, that occupied and sometimes collided with our two bodies proved way more interesting than the conversation we shared. My internal clock ticked and tocked; the subtle gestures, the roaming eye contact, the awkwardness, my nervousness, because it really was just a matter of time. We sat first opposite each other at a stone-cold wooden booth but after getting our first beers from the bar, upon his return, Nick sat next to me and, well, the rest is history. The only bartender excused himself, saying that he'd be back, had to wrap things up downstairs or something. He closed the doors, locking us in for the most part, and when his footsteps faded Nick wasted no time, leaning into me, pushing my body so that my back was against the wall and my either side was harnessed by the table on my right and the back of my seat on the left. His first kiss was a near assault, but the sloppiness was apropos. A little animalesque if I can be so bold. I pushed him away, not want-ing to kiss like that in a place like this. Without words, he got the hint and helped me again, out from my seat, then went ahead and un-locked the door to the bar. We were streetside in no time.

"My place is about a ten-minute walk from here," he groaned in my ear. I bit my lip, desperate not to unleash a giggle, a cackle, or a random remark. As much as my body had one objective, my mind couldn't help but remind me of how cliché this really all was.

"I'm right around the corner," I said. Body wins.

It was me who led the way, me who for a moment or so loved the power of such spontaneity. I loved making out in the vacant stairway of my building once we were sure no one was around. I loved being felt up with the speed and roughness of a nervous kid in the seventh grade. I loved that we couldn't make our minds up fast enough: Swap it up in the alcove or take the time to get up to my apartment. Naughty, raw, hilarious—it was all good fun. And I'd be lying if I didn't admit that I thought about Jack from time to time and smiled inside knowing full well that he would be so upset by this en-tire display. But it was all fun and games until Nick got in. Once in my apartment, the truth trickled as loudly as a leaky faucet in the mid-dle of the night.

It was a relief to feel wanted again. It was great to know that my immediate attraction to Nick when I'd met him on day one was reciprocated. This, it, he, I thought, would be just what the doctor ordered for my mangled little heart. But it wasn't. It was like over-the-counter cold medicine. It numbs you, gives you a pseudo-high even—but it doesn't help you get better.

Enter Nick: with two cups of coffee and a pack of Camel Lights in his hand.

"Hey," he said. "Anyone sitting here?"

Shocked. "Hey. No. No one, sit down."

"He told me I'd find you here," he said quietly.

"Who?" I said.

"The coffee guy on the corner. Good guy."

"Yeah. I usually get—"

"Light and sweet," he said and handed me a coffee. "Two Sweet'n Lows."

"Yup."

"Every single morning on your way here."

"Exactly," I said. Shyly. I was feeling better. He was shaping up to be a pretty decent guy.

"Don't feel all weird about last night, okay?" he assured me.

"Oh, oh, well, well, I'm not. I'm fine with it," I said rather unconvincingly.

"Yeah. Well, I had a great time." He struggled trying to peel back the plastic opening on the lid. "You were incredible."

"Here," I said, grabbing the cup and doing it for him, dying inside. You'd think it would feel somewhat gratifying to hear that I got two thumbs-up. Not so. All I thought was, *Oh my God, I don't even know his last name!*

"I was so stoked when I saw you on that bus last night, Vivian. I had been hoping to run into you one of these days."

"Yeah?"

"Totally."

I nodded. This bit of information did strike a chord with my happy place.

"You are such a cute-ee." With that he kissed me on my forehead and got up.

I smiled and wanted to purr in the way I imagined May's little Smitten would.

"I'm going out of town today. But I left my info on your dresser, just in case I didn't find you."

"Where ya going?" I asked.

"Vegas. But I'll be back in a few weeks and I'm gonna track you down if I don't hear from you. You got me?"

"Yes."

Again, he repeated, "You got me?"

"Yeah, sure."

"Promise me."

"I promise."

I would have enjoyed that little exchange a bit more had I not been distracted, aware of a few uptighters standing to my left. I imagined bringing Nick home to meet my parents, insisting all through dinner that he not remove the gloves I made him wear!

Maybe I freaked out too soon. Maybe not. But his visit and his remarks made me feel a whole lot better. Maybe I was built for pseudo-TLC. Scary thought, eh?

fifteen

Days became weeks and weeks, disguised, turned into months. The summer was long gone and Christmas was so underwhelming that I've decided to skip it. On a brighter note, Jayden was back in my life. She had up and left for Seattle and as I tripped my way through a series of temps, and before I had fallen in love with any of them, she was back in my office, carrying a whole bunch of beads in her hand and streams of tears down her face. I made my best efforts not to gloat as she begged for her job back and, well, so far so good.

Noteworthy: May and Daniel were now public, Sheryl was recently engaged, and, only recently, Sophie and Rob were now sharing the same address. There hadn't been anyone in my life since Nick and no, I hadn't heard from him again. But that was all right. I didn't sweat it. He had left the ball in my court and I made the decision to keep the reference appropriate. O.N.S.

My first novel was weeks away from its debut and I had yet to start the second. Instead I spent most of my free time at the office and then at the gym. I tossed off the extra poundage with my most recent obsession: kickboxing. The perfect exercise regimen for those of us with lots of "stuff." Besides being a ridiculous cardio mechanism, punching and kicking is the best way to tell off anyone (in your mind of course) that you ever needed to. I virtually kicked the ass of every shit I ever dated, every boss I ever hated, and even let my bikini waxer have it on one or two separate occasions. The gym, for me, was not an extracurricular social setting. Instead of batting my eyelashes on a StairMaster somewhere or displaying my limberness in a crowded yoga class, I'd stake out an abandoned corner, push a sand-based freestanding heavy bag there, and, with an iPod ready-equipped with all the Notorious B.I.G. I could rip, I boxed and kicked away.

The only downside was keeping my new skills at bay. There were many evenings, walking down the streets, getting nudged by passersby, being bumped into in crowded aisles of a supermarket, when I fully felt like one of Brad Pitt's disciples in *Fight Club*. Wasn't that easy to turn off that fighting spirit, but I utilized it in different ways in time.

"Vivian," Jayden announced through the intercom, "you've got Victoria on line one."

"Hey Victoria," I said cautiously. The sound of her name came with its own scary movie soundtrack. "What's up?"

"I've got news, sweetcakes."

"Oh boy," I said as I sat straight up at my desk. "What?"

"You want the good or the bad first?"

"The bad." What good was good news to me if I knew that something bad was right behind it?

"Your reviews came in, two of them."

Deadpan: "Oh-my-God."

"Relax, honey. They're not that bad. Well, yes, yes they are. But it doesn't matter. You know what? I shouldn't have told you . . . WHAT?" she barked. "Hang on a second . . ."

I heard Victoria scream in the background, "You did WHAT? Why Stephanie, why? I specifically told you not to fax them to her!"

Enter Jayden: "Viv, this just came in for you."

"Vivian? Vivian? Are you there?"

I was, physically anyway. But mentally, I had already shot myself in the head.

"Vivian . . . Vivian?"

"I'm here."

"You're reading them, aren't you?"

"Now will you fire her?" I whined. "Please?"

"Consider it done, sweetcakes. Now listen . . ."

"Yeah . . ."

"Seriously, will you listen to me. The reviews mean shit to me and shit to everyone else who matters, so let's move on."

"Fine."

"Rip them up, Vivian."

"Fine."

"I mean it. Tear them up. On the phone, now, or I'll promote her."

I put the phone on SPEAKER and I tore up an interoffice memo from Stan that detailed our revised expense-account protocols. "Done," I said.

"Very good. So, now then, the good news. To whom should I direct option inquiries?"

"What?"

"To whom should I direct option inquiries?"

"No, I heard you. I just don't know what you mean."

"Okay," she said impatiently. "Do you remember when we did a mailing of your galleys?"

"My what?"

"You better not still be reading those reviews, Vivian!"

"I'm not." I was.

"Your galleys. The first printing of your manuscript that we send to members of the press and such."

"Yeah, yeah, now I remember."

"Well, and now you'll see why two crap reviews mean nothing,

I've got three messages from production companies and one from an agency that want to talk to you about optioning your book."

And there went my lunch. Those damn shwarma sandwiches! They do me in every time! "You're kidding," I gasped.

"No, Vivian, I'm not. Now will you please snap out of it and listen!"

"I'm listening."

"This is major. You need to follow up ASAP. These people in L.A. have A.D.D. in the worst—"

"—W.A.Y."

"Shut it, will you!"

Laughing, I said, "This just doesn't seem real."

"Well, it is. It's the ideal opportunity for any writer, Vivian. I'll e-mail you their numbers and you'll have to do the rest."

"Gotcha."

"And don't think I've forgotten about that second manuscript. You've got sixteen weeks, sweetcakes."

"Thank you, Victoria."

"Bye-bye."

" 'Bye."

I hung up and immediately, it was as if I was seeing everything around me for the first time. Nothing in my office looked familiar. There was now a new challenge obstructing my view. Sure, I wanted to jump out of my seat, race down the hall, screaming and jumping like a lottery winner, like a girl who just got a kiss and an autograph and a photo with Tom Cruise, like a baseball player, on the winning side, after the third out of the ninth inning in a World Series game seven, but I wasn't that inclined. Because I was completely freaking out. It couldn't be this easy? Or could it? But I knew better deep down inside: Nothing ever was.

I took a few deep breaths and picked up the receiver but it was like a freeze-frame moment . . . who to call?

My parents would have a million questions, to which I would have zero answers, and then call everyone they knew and exaggerate. I could hear it already: *Vivian's life is being turned into a movie!* Okay, next. Sophie was away with Rob; telling May (during office hours) was too risky, as I wasn't ready for anyone at work to know; and, well, that left my big brother Joseph, who would, of course, act like a big brother and question and advise me to death.

Hmmmm.

Receiver down.

I checked my e-mail, and no message was delivered yet, so I decided to pack it up early and make my way home. Sit on the news for the night and deal with it come morning.

I was in shock, is all. Why else would I not have reacted to something so surreal?

Just out of the subway and on my way home, my mind was somewhere else. I was alert enough, however, to observe yet another small shop in Nolita in what was now a familiar going-out-of-business mode. These incredible tiny shops with amazing clothing were everywhere. A candy store for fashionistas is what my neighborhood was like. And so, of course, there was a vulturous crowd filled with women just like you and me who had the space jam-packed. Devouring the remaining discounted merchandise, girls were leaving multibagged with looks of complete satisfaction. Well, there was no stopping me.

The selection was piecemeal but I didn't mind much for just above every long rack was a giant acid-green cardboard sign with Sharpie so fresh you could smell it that read: 60% OFF SALE PRICE—CASH ONLY. This was so my kind of store. Having learned from the best, Sophie, I stayed close to the dressing rooms, waiting for my chance to pick through the piles of discards on the floor. When a girl with a build similar to mine finally exited, I dashed right in. And just as Sophie had always predicted, a slew of fab frocks awaited my perusal.

Miraculously, the one garment that I worshipped and that also fit me like a glove, a gorg striped Cameron-Diaz-ish dress, designer unknown, was marked down to, if my mathematical mind served me, $120. Done!!! I exited the fitting room victorious and plopped my proud almost-purchase on the counter. I say *almost* because when I went to grab my wallet, it was nowhere to be found. Making matters momentarily worse, the chick behind me offered to take the dress off the shop owner's hands without even trying it on and before I could plead to have her hold it, for $140. Realizing there were more impending serious issues at stake, I could only growl at her as I walked away, defeated yet really panicked. I was sure that I had not left the wallet at the office. I knew this because I had grabbed it to get my MetroCard for the subway just fifteen minutes before.

Outside the store, I rifled through my purse for my cell phone. Also gone. It was then that I had realized I had been pickpocketed and I completely tweaked out! It's an incredibly alarming sensation. You feel so violated and yet so stupid not to have seen or felt the crime.

Just as I was making up my mind—*police or credit card company?*—that wench who'd stolen my dress passed by me and smiled. *What goes around comes around,* I repeated to myself as I walked over to the phone booth, found some loose change, and called American Express. And although I was able to cancel the card almost immediately, someone had already gone shopping, to the tune of nearly six hundred dollars. Same deal with Visa, but worse, nine hundred.

Where's a freestanding heavyweight bag when you really need one???

Okay. Now this was definitely a big-brother scenario.

"How come I only hear from you when you need something, Vivian?" he said rather condescendingly.

"Please Joseph. Just come get me. I'm a wreck."

"Hang in there. It's going to take me about thirty minutes. You had to call me now, at rush hour?" Joseph was now a Park Slope (Brooklyn) man. A friend had offered him his one-bedroom apartment as he would be leaving NYC for a year, and with rents in this city higher than any stiletto Mr. Choo could come up with, Joseph packed his bags without a second thought.

"Yup, Joe, I did. I asked the pickpocket to rob me blind during rush hour just 'cause I wanted to piss you off."

"Should I just meet you at your place? Do you still have your keys?"

"Shit. Good question. Hang on . . . Yes."

"See you in thirty . . . at your place." He huffed and hung up.

It was strange to be without a cell phone or a dollar. Strange scary, not strange different. It marked the first time in a long time that I'd felt like a tourist. Like the Pennsylvania girl I was when I'd arrived here. Not the city slicker I had thought that I'd become.

sixteen

Joseph and I had what started out as a quiet dinner at a great Chinese place in Gramercy—after, of course, about two hours' worth of drama, complete with police reports and all.

"So what's with you and this single-white-female shit? Are you dating anyone?"

"No," I said defensively. "Are you?"

"Do you even have to ask?" he smugged.

"Uch. No. I forgot that your office is across the street from the High School for Performing Arts." I sang, *"Fame! I'm gonna live forever. I'm gonna learn how to fly! High! I'm gonna . . ."*

"Save it." He smiled. "What about Jack? Have you heard from him?"

"I feel it coming to—"

"Irene Cara . . . you big freak. I'm serious. Have you?"

"No." I tried to hide my automatic pout.

"You really fucked up that one, I tell ya."

"Thanks, Joe." I decided to fill him in on Victoria's big call earlier that afternoon—a definite change of subject that I knew would not lead to more of his collective romantic wisdom.

Agasp, he mumbled, "Are you joking?" with a mouthful of moo shu.

"No."

"Did you tell Mom and Dad?"

"No."

"Good call there," he joked. "So who ya gonna call?"

"Ghostbusters."

"Seriously"—laughing—"what's wrong with you?"

I confided, "Honestly Joe, I can only imagine that if New York is cutthroat, the entertainment business must be a nightmare."

He nearly dropped his egg roll. "Vivian, please. This coming from the same girl who jumped, no, wait, spun around a few times first, and then jumped off the porch in her red underwear and Mom's gold belt, only to give Nana a heart attack and lose your TV privileges for a month, because you tried to prove that you really were Wonder Woman's little sister and then you, astonishingly enough, actually lived to tell about it?"

"Shut up."

"Same girl who learned how to play poker with me and Dad and actually take us for twenty dollars, each, when you were, what . . . all of nine years old?"

"I'm not kidding, Joseph!"

"Vivian. You came to New York and did all of this on your own—"

"I know but I was naive."

"Listen to me," he urged. "Besides being born a contemptuous little pill, Mom's words, not mine of course, you were born fearless. You manage to pull off anything you set your mind to. It's your instinct and probably your only redeeming quality."

"Thanks, Joseph."

"Don't worry about it."

Joe's cell phone rang. He licked a few fingers clean and picked it up. "Hey Mom," he said, looking at me with a dare.

No. No. No! I mouthed.

"Did Vivian tell you—"

"No."

"She was pickpocketed."

"Jerk."

"Yup. Yup. Huh-huh. Yup."

I got up to leave.

"Hang on, Ma. Where you going?"

"Home."

"Sit down! You don't even have any money."

"Yeah I do . . . Check your wallet. I grabbed a few twenties when you went to tinkle."

"Wait a—"

"Love ya," I said and kissed him on the cheek. I retrieved my jacket from the coat-check girl and made my way home.

Joseph was such the big brother and every now and then I let him indulge me with his words of wisdom and assumed sage advice. But he was right where Hollywood was concerned. I needed to ignore the hiccups in my belly and get on with it. Half-assing anything at this point would all but cancel out everything else I had worked so hard for. And making this option thing a *no-big-deal* thing to me and everyone else would have been a huge cop-out. I decided to confide in Sheryl first. Of everyone I knew who was connected in that world, she was the only one, I was sure, who wouldn't feed me to the wolves.

The streets were packed, and, being very close to Irving Plaza, it was not very sleuth-ee of me to surmise that a concert must have just let out. It was now, of course, that I thought about and then went to zip up my purse. When I remembered that it was basically empty, I just left it as is and frowned.

It was while I was still eyeing my bag that I was bumped. And a man's voice said, "Oh excuse . . . us." And when I looked up, there was Jack and I thought I'd been dreaming. It was like nothing had changed and we were about to kiss. Staring up at him, him looking down at me. Silence. But then I saw a bit of Grace and was sure it was a nightmare and then I heard, "Viv! Vivian!" and I turned and it was May with Daniel and I said "hey" and when I turned again, Jack (and Grace) were gone.

"Hey mama!"

I smirked.

"Boy, someone is a little snarky," she teased.

"Hi Vivian," Daniel said.

"Hey . . . did you see?" I said faintishly.

"Who?" May asked.

"You didn't see . . ."

"Who?" Daniel said.

"That wasn't . . ."

"Who?" she said again, looking around a sea of fresh faces.

"Forget it."

"Are you all right?" she asked, grabbing my hand.

"I'm fine. I'm just tired. How was the concert? Who was play-ing?"

"Sting! Can you even believe? He was amazing!"

"Wow."

"Yeah, Stan had two extra tickets. I went to see if you wanted to go and you had left early. I called you on your cell phone but it was disconnected. Did you forget to pay your bill again?"

"No, no. Long story. I'll pop over to your desk in the morning. It's all good."

"You sure?" May asked.

"Do you want to join us for sushi?" offered Daniel.

"I'm fine, and so sweet of you to ask, Daniel, but I just had din-ner. Chinese."

We said our good-byes, hugged, and I kept walking till I was sure they were gone. Then I leaned on a parked car and ignited its alarm so I dashed and found a security-free park bench and parked it.

What had just happened? I knew it was him (them). I wasn't that far gone that I was now hallucinating. Uch, he looked good, you guys. Granted I just saw his face but it looked good. It looked perfect. And I should point out that he, too, looked like he'd seen a ghost. I wondered why he didn't stick around. Did he not care? Did he not want to be bothered? Was she a big jealous freak inside a perfect tiny body? Maybe she pushed him ahead? So many questions and so much time to sweat over each of them.

But then I got angry. We had spent so many great years together fight-free. And we broke up, fine. But it had been like forever already. He can't suck it up and find a "hello" for me? What's that about? Do you know how sick I felt inside when he was gone? I felt discarded. I felt chumped.

I noticed one of those street posters on the floor below me. I picked it up, and there was Sting with a fresh boot stain on his face. I turned it over and it was still white, for all intents and purposes clean, and I followed my next instinct, grabbed a pen from my bag, and, leaning on the bench's back, I wrote . . .

Dear Jack, That was you tonight, wasn't it? I miss you. I have some things I want to tell you. Things that I want you to know. Please call me. Vivian

What harm was a harmless olive branch? I walked over to the firehouse that he'd been at for the last seven years, figuring the odds were pretty high he was still working there. It was a solid fourteen blocks and three avenues away, but my heart was pumping and I didn't even consider that a distraction. I thought about the repercussions and I didn't much care. Was I ready to talk to him? That didn't much matter 'cause I was so overthinking about him day in and day out. Was I ready to get back with him? Completely. Did I think about Grace and how she might be in the way? Not for a second. I truly believed that no matter whom he was seeing, he'd always have a place in his heart for me. Yes, of course, the fact that she was every ex-girlfriend's worst nightmare did make me feel awful but in the end I didn't think it would count.

The "V" Spot

The closer I got to the firehouse, the more nervous I began to feel. And when I saw two boys (no more than twelve) playing something or other a few yards away from the station, I called them over and offered them ten bucks to hand-deliver my letter. I had only a twenty, so they excitedly escorted me to the grocery store where I got change and convinced the clerk to sell me an envelope. Which he didn't have, so I went with the next best thing, a paper bag. I folded up my poster-slash-letter, placed it neatly inside the bag, wrote Jack's name on the outside, and rolled the top over just so. I gave my accomplices fast directions, requesting that they leave the bag for "Jack Victor," making sure to hand it off to someone trustworthy. The plan was that I'd sit on the corner, guard their bikes, and give them the balance, five bucks, when they snuck back and gave me a full report. And yes, that's right, five bucks. They insisted on securing half in advance. "My dad's a lawyer," one boy relayed smartly. "I know these things."

I smiled and shooed them ahead.

Moments later they skipped back, palms outstretched, and I made good on my offer. "Tony," the other boy relayed. "We gave it to Tony and I said Jack Victor and when he asked me who sent him I pointed you out."

"Oh, did you?"

"Yup."

Great.

seventeen

I didn't sleep much that night. Sure, I was waiting for the phone to ring miraculously, or, yes, I'll admit it, to hear the gentle taps of an acorn or stone against my window. But neither occurred. Making matters worse, Omelet had gas (bad bad gas) and my neighbors were passionately fighting and then passionately making up. I didn't think to take two Tylenol PMs until way past midnight, so waking up the next morning was rough.

May beat me to the punch and paid me an A.M. visit and nearly fell off her chair when I thoroughly caught her up. From my conversation with Victoria to the pickpocketing to the Jack sighting and the packed-lunch-like letter.

"Well, you certainly have enough shit going on to fill the pages of all these damn books!" she joked, trying (desperately) to find a plus side. "Seriously, V, what are you going to do . . . if he doesn't call?"

"That's not an option, May, right? It's just not." The more I said that, the more I hoped to believe it.

Uncomfortable, as I'm sure (now that I'm able to look back at that conversation) I exposed more desperation and earnestness than she'd anticipated, she (very) delicately continued, "Honey, I'm just going to say this because I'd expect the same honesty from you . . . okay?"

"Just be gentle," I replied sarcastically.

"I hope he does call. I really really do. And I for one think he will but"—she emphasized—"you broke that boy's heart."

"I know." I sniffed apologetically.

"And that sometimes—not always, but sometimes—causes lasting effects, especially with men, and erects these like superhuman walls of steel." She saw me shrivel up and came back strong. "But I still think he's going to come around and call you. Just give him some time."

"Thanks baby."

"Of course."

Without knocking and very much out of nowhere, which was just so Sheryl, she jumped into my office and barked, "We have to talk about your message . . . like now." She sat herself atop my desk before I could sneak a word in edgewise, gestured for me to open my window, flipped off her latest and greatest pair of shiny black Manolo Blahniks, knotted her stick-straight shellacked hair in a makeshift pony, lit up her cig-ee, and got straight to it. "I have a friend. From grade school. A real friend." Puff. Puff. "She's a writer in Los Angeles. She hasn't done much but her brother's been"—Puff. Puff—"successful and more importantly, her husband runs"—Puff—"Agent Jar Films." Puff.

May: "Oh my gosh—they're huge."

Sheryl: "Uh, yup?!?"

I looked at May in a very don't-be-offended-it's-just-Sheryl way and at the same time regretfully slid my practically brand-new vanilla skim latte beneath her hand as a makeshift ashtray.

Without as much as a flinch or a thank-you she continued. "Anyway, with your permission, I'd like to call her, send her this galley, and get her opinion."

"That's fine with me, Sher. Anything you could do would be—"

"Okay. Consider it done. Maybe I'll just call her now and tell her to look out for the manuscript. Can you get someone over there"—she meant at the publisher's—"to overnight it to her?"

"I think so."

"Good. I'll e-mail you all her info." She flicked her cigarette in my poor undeserving latte and made her exit.

"Jesus she's intense," May quipped.

"Oh, I know!" I sang while happily and virtually crossing GET CONTACT IN CALIFORNIA off my to-do list.

May heard Stan whining for her in the background and whispered, "Some things never change." And got up to leave. "Hey listen," she remembered. "We have to get Sophie and Rob something."

"We do?" I asked.

"Sure, like a housewarming gift."

"Oh."

She took a cue from my response, I gathered, and generously replied, "You want me to take care of it?"

And I nodded with a half smile.

She winked and left to play with the sharks.

Back to the drawing board, I thought, and flipped my computer on to start the day, officially. I raced through my e-mails, deleting offer after offer to MAKE MY PENIS LONGER, and made sure to catch myself up on the day's current events, i.e., gossip alerts and fashion forecasts. (I'm all about being in the know.)

Enter Stan: "What have I said about smoking in the office, Vivian?"

"I—"

"I can't bend that rule for Your Highness—"

"I wasn't—oh forget it. What's up?" I said bitterly.

"Did you read Drew's e-mail?" he asked pleasantly.

"No. Not yet. I haven't gotten to it. Why?"

"He, er, we heard back from Hawk yesterday. We came looking for you and then we tried your cell phone—"

"I—"

"It doesn't matter. The point is, he thinks he can get us a deal."

"You're kidding?" I said.

"Do I ever?" he queened. Sorry, explained.

"Read it, talk to Drew, and put something on my calendar. This is big."

To catch you up, for the past year we'd been trying to break into the music business. Not in a Britney, or Clay Aiken kind of way, but rather to redefine the compilation business. Hawk was our facilitator, agent if you will, a hotshot manager who had been in the business in a big way for years and years. Drew, May, Sheryl, and I had spent more evenings than any of us cared to remember putting presentations together, then mornings, afternoons, and even evenings, dancing, pitching our hearts out, trying to get the music industry to embrace a new way of selling and marketing music. After taking meeting after meeting, running into executive after executive who all claimed they wanted change but didn't have the balls to bite, on the advice of Hawk we then let the whole thing "breathe" for a bit. So this, Stan's update, was fully out of the blue.

So I scrolled down and found Drew's message, which confirmed everything that Stan had said. According to Hawk, a major record label was (finally) interested. They liked that the publishing world had embraced us and were willing to dive in. Off the low board. And there were rules. They (label) had final approval of nearly everything, and we would have one shot. If the first Vivianlives compilation record performed, there could be up to five more. But if it didn't, the deal was dead. Plain and simple.

"I'll take it!" was my response to Drew and all cc'd parties. "What do we have to lose?"

"Only everything," Sheryl responded first. "If we don't maintain creative control and if there's not an ample budget, which it doesn't sound like there will be, then we're doomed."

"You're being dramatic, Sheryl," Drew chimed in. "This is a major opportunity. If the record tanks, they're to blame, not us, and we can go back out there and find a new label and learn from our mistakes."

"Vivian?" Stan replied. Which was shocking. Did he (Stan) not want to be the scapegoat if we landed on our asses? Was that why he failed to respond? Why he was, apparently, leaving it up to me? Hmmmmm.

"I say we do it. I agree with both Sheryl and Drew, but if we don't stick our necks out, we'll never know."

From Stan: "Drew, set it up."

From Drew: "Done."

Now this was getting goooooood.

Jayden on intercom: "Vivian?"

"Yeah?"

"I've got Jack-a"—HOLY SHIT!—"-lyn on line two for you."

Wait? What?

"Who?" I asked.

"Jacquelyn," she repeated. "She says she's a friend of Sheryl's?"

"Okay. Give me a second."

False alarm. ☹

I picked up. "Hi Jacquelyn."

"Vivian Livingston! I just got off the phone with Shoe-Shoe."

God, that was quick, I thought but wasn't too surprised. This was Sheryl we were dealing with.

"Shoe-Shoe?"

"That's my pet name for Sheryl. She calls me Jacks, you should probably get used to it."

"Oh . . . I'll try." Eek. If I have to.

"Sheryl's told me so much about you. We're all anxiously awaiting your novel! How exciting. Ten days or so, right?"

"Yes. Right. Thank you. That's very sweet, Jacquelyn," I said.

"Please," she said, "call me Jacks, I insist."

I took a deep breath and replied as gracefully as I could, "Okay, Jacks."

Oye.

All in all Jacquelyn was very kind and generous. She briefed me on the ways of her world and what the process of "optioning" a novel would be like. What to watch out for, what to ask for, what to insist on, and the range, monetarily, of what to aim for. I completely took notes. She also extended an offer. She would call a few agents and tell them about me and if any were interested, she would have them call me directly. She prefaced that she would make sure I was in good hands and gave me her contact information, saying that I could call or e-mail her whenever if I had any questions or wanted her take on something or someone. "It's L.A. baby," she ended. "You need all the friends you can get."

Ladies, we have liftoff.

eighteen

The book would debut in ten days and counting, and with seven long gone I still had received not a word from Jack. The first few days were horrific. Especially with "Jacks" calling me twelve times a day. Honestly, you guys, I was developing a twitch. Omelet was also way under the weather. We traipsed to the vet on three separate occasions and all they could do for him was prescribe an animal-friendly Imodium-esque product and bill me seventy-five bucks a pop.

All that aside, I was back in workwoman mode, a very welcome distraction. I was too busy to be freaking out about what was in store. Victoria, Stephanie (V's still-employed evil assistant), Jayden, and Sheryl were frantically planning my book tour, I was having hypernatural conversations with Hollywood executives and then translating them with, well, you know who (on her West Coast time), *and* it looked like Mr. Hawk was really a man of his word. Legal was now busy deciphering a lengthy contract from the record label and a pseudo-friendly get-acquainted meeting with everyone, on both sides, who would be working on album number one was scheduled for the following week. Apparently that was how confident they were about closing our deal. A giant meeting on the calendar be-fore completed paperwork—an observation handed down to me from Drew—was a very very good sign.

May and I went for lunch that day, I remember. We vowed to not discuss anything work-related as, these days, it seemed that was all we ever talked about. We chose a quasi-health-food restaurant and fine, I didn't eat anything fried, but because I was served up a small plate of starved vegetation, I engulfed a loaf or three of bread instead.

She talked a lot about Daniel. They had a big vacation planned for Memorial Day weekend, her mother and sister adored him, they were thinking of getting Smitten a brother or sister. It was all rainbows and roses in May's la-la land. And I was happy for her and I really liked him so my responses, both articulated and thought, were genuine.

It was over dessert, a fruit cup, that she broached the taboo topic. "He still hasn't called, has he?"

"Nope."

"And how are you with it?"

"Fifty–fifty. I'm as hurt as I am pissed off."

"That's valid, V."

"Why thanks, Doc," I blipped.

"Hey!"

"Sorry."

"Ya know, maybe you're just lonely and really vulnerable right now. You're about to enter a whole new phase of your life and there's no one there, you know, at home. Did you ever think about that, V? Maybe it's not Jack as much as it's the idea of a Jack?"

"Listen, May, you're right about all of it. I am lonely. I do wish I had someone to go through and share all this with. And for a while, a very long while, I didn't think it was Jack that I wanted. That I needed. That I missed. But ya know what?"

"What?"

"It so is." And I started to cry. She came over to my side of the booth to comfort me and then my waitress offered to run outside and find me something fried, having noted that I didn't exactly bask in the au naturel environment, and I thought that was exceptionally nice.

"I can't believe I'm going to say this to you because it really goes against my better judgment, but why not try again?"

"Huh?" I sniffed, wiping my wrist past my nose, upsetting my neighbors, no doubt.

"Maybe Jack doesn't buy it. Maybe he's afraid. I mean, maybe he thinks that you're not serious and that this all has to do with his mega-babe."

"Hey?"

"What? I've never seen her. That was your catchphrase, honey, not mine."

I took a deep breath. "So what are you saying?"

"Call him. Send an invite, maybe, for the book signing to his apartment."

"Are you mad?"

"No, why?"

"I could barely breathe when I saw him the night of the Sting concert. Now I'm going to ask him to sit front-row center at my signing where I'm expected to enunciate?"

"Good point. Fine. Then call him. My first suggestion. Here," she said, handing me her cell phone. (I still hadn't picked up mine.)

"No!"

"Why?"

"No! Are you crazy? Here? Now?"

"Why? You scared?"

"Don't dare me, May!" I laughed/cried/sniffled/smiled.

"I'm not."

"Are too."

"Am not."

"Are too."

"Am not!"

"Shut up!" I laughed/cried/giggled/sniffed. "Give it to me."

Oh, does she know me . . .

I dialed Jack's number as both May and our waitress, Amy, sat and held hands and prayed.

Ringing.

"What?" May yelped. "What's going on???"

"Still ringing," I reported.

"Should she leave a message?" Amy mentioned as she and I both looked at May for a decision.

"Yes!" May shrieked.

The message played . . .

"Hi this is Jack . . . and Grace!" (Her voice.) *"We're not here right now. Leave a message."* Beep.

I hung up and from the looks on my friend and new friend's faces, there was something in the color of my skin that said, *Not good.*

"She answered," May predicted.

"He moved?" Amy hoped.

"They live together."

They both shook their heads and then raised their hands in the air. So in unison that I was sure that they were either fraternal twins separated at birth or had choreographed it. And I chuckled.

May said, "Screw that, V, call back and leave a message!"

Amy added, "They probably have caller something-or-other anyway, so you kind of have to. One hang-up before a message could be normal. Like bad reception or something."

"Yeah," May concurred.

I wanted to leave a message. A big fat juicy message that would either-slash-both piss Grace off, get Jack in trouble, or, optimally, cause a raging fight that would force Jack to run to me for my broad shoulders!

But I didn't. It just didn't seem right. Soon after, we invited Amy to my signing, paid the bill, and walked back to the office.

"One small step . . . ," May added. "At least you dealt with it. You did something."

"True . . . but enough already. What else is up, May? Change the subject, would ya? Please? I'm so damn melancholy I feel like we just ate a bunch of 'em in our salads!"

"Well, I wasn't going to bring it up, because I know we both promised—"

"I have no idea what you're talking about," I said.

"Yeah right!" she laughed.

"I don't!" I insisted.

"Oh, you're good. You're good. Youuuuu." She was doing her best-and-overdone impression of Robert De Niro in *Analyze This*.

"Quit it!" I whined. And I think she finally believed me because she looked like a little version of herself caught with one, no, both of her hands in the cookie jar.

"Forget I said anything," she mumbled awkwardly.

"No! What are you talking about?"

"Forget it!" she begged.

"No way girl . . . spill!"

"You mean to tell me Rob didn't call you last weekend?"

"Noooooooo," I said rather frantically.

"Fuck."

"Fuck what?"

"Fuck."

"Fuck what May? You are freaking me out right now! Fuck what?"

She stopped walking and could barely look me in the eye. "Well, Rob called me—"

"I know! You said that already."

"Shhhhhh! Rob called me and, to make a long story short, asked me to meet him at Tiffany's tomorrow, after work—"

"Oh—my—God—May. PLEASE TELL ME HE WANTS TO GET HER A CHARM BRACELET!!!"

"Nope."

"Not one of those cute silver link bracelets, with the heart?"

She shook her head.

"With the toggle?"

She shook her head.

I shook mine.

"I'm so sorry, V. I just assumed he had called and asked you, too."

"Nope." My blood was boiling.

"I thought you didn't say anything because, well, because he asked you not to. Like he did me."

"Nope."

"Hey, I'm sure it's just an oversight."

"Oh no, I'm so sure it wasn't. Where I'm from, May, we call that a snub."

"I don't think so, really I—"

I grabbed her hand. "Listen. I'm not mad. At you. It's okay."

She looked at me skeptically.

"Okay, it's not okay," I admitted. "But there's nothing I'm going to do about it so it has to be . . . okay . . . all right?"

"Okay."

"So please please please do not mention it to him. Don't bring it up. Just be cool, all right?"

"All right. [Pause.] But I feel terrible."

"Don't. [Pause.] You go on ahead. I need to take a few."

"You sure?"

"Yeah, go on. I'll see you back up there in a little while."

And she complied, warily.

I wandered and it began to rain. The first dry space was a random shoe store and I entered and sat there and ignored the three salesmen who asked if I needed any help, in their orthopedic special-needs custom shoe shop, and I said no, thank you, and they, generously, let me be. (For the time being.)

I thought that this had to be the most blatantly disrespectful blow that anyone had ever hit me with. I knew this cat didn't like me. We'd never really hit it off. He just never seemed interested. And that was fine. He didn't have to. We could coexist in Sophie's life, for better or for worse, for richer or for poorer, in sickness and in health until the day that Sophie had their marriage annulled. Right?

I worked hard at not taking Sophie's recent disappearance personally, knowing full well where she was and why. And on many many levels, I was happy for her. But for Rob to not include me and to call on May, well, that was just caustic. It reeked, to me at least, of ownership and insecurity and a big fat *fuck you*. And my hands were tied. What was I going to do? Wreck Sophie's experience? Cause tension? I couldn't. I had to bite it, be bigger than him and get over it.

Mount Everest would be easier to climb.

And that's when I decided to call Jack. (Again.) Rob brought out my fighting spirit and if that was what I had to do to get through to him, fight for him, to let him know and feel that I was for real, well, then, so be it.

I borrowed the shoe shop's rotary phone and got the answering machine, had the distinct pleasure of listening to "their" message again, and jumped in, headfirst:

"Hi Jack. It's Vivian. Could you call me? Not on my cell, I, I lost it. Either at home or at work. No. Wait. I didn't lose my phone at home or at work. I meant, call me at home or at work. Okay? Great. Thanks. I wanted to talk to you. Thanks! 'Bye! Bye-bye."

Smooooooooth.

And then: "Miss? I brought these out for you."

Huh?

I looked up and there was a wiry figure with a comb-over and bad teeth in a shrunken navy-ish suit who smelled like tuna fish.

"Did you know that difficulties like swelling, bunions, corns, or hammertoes threaten feet, especially those with diabetes, and pose a risk for developing further foot problems?"

"No. NO I didn't."

He grinned, very self-pleased. Then added, "That's what I thought. Allow me to explain: These added-depth shoes from Brooks"—showing me the orthopedics—"enable you to surround your sensitive feet with ample protection. The wide, broad toe, total contact dual-density insole to absorb shock and redistribute pressure, soft foam-padded tongue and collar, and wide shank for excellent lateral stability will provide you with unprecedented foot comfort. Have a look: There's even adjustable Velcro straps. Soft calf leather . . ."

Fast-forward twenty minutes: I handed him my (new) credit card and had a size seven shipped to my nana.

Nineteen

Rob proposed to Sophie the night of my book signing and she never made it there. Not her fault, I am fully aware of that, I mean, how would she know of his plans? She didn't. Although I am certain that Rob knew, as he and about six of his fraternity friends happened to RSVP to the cocktail reception that followed the signing session at the bookstore. (Deep breaths here.) And Jack did not dignify my two attempts at contacting him with even the slightest response and with my parents, my nana (new shoes and all), my brother, my cousins and aunts and uncles, all in town for the occasion, dominating the first four rows in the audience, and every other friend, acquaintance, coworker I could remember showing full support, too, it was a very good thing that Sheryl had thought to bring a few minis along. Which I threw back in the public bathroom in the children's section of the store just minutes beforehand. She didn't exactly have to twist my arm, either.

Having to read from my novel, sign books, and greet guests all there on my behalf was an exercise in futility. Granted, it got way easier in time, but this was night one. I was riddled with insecurity—so much so, I had a hard time reading. My vision blurred, every pore dripped with sweat, and my voice even began to crack on a few occasions. (It was afterward that I realized that I might have to cross ACTRESS off any future goals list.)

It was, however, a dream realized. Seeing my novel, hundreds of them, in the windows of bookstores, in city after city, in airport after airport, receiving praise from readers, seeing my mother's face beam from the crowd, was a thrill and a feeling that is difficult to put into words. And it was that night that I made sure to feel it, through and through—the admiration, the love, and the support from loved ones, old and new.

Sophie phoned me at the after-party while I was knee-deep in champagne to congratulate me, apologize, and give me the great news. I winged it. I was leaving in the morning for a twelve-city book tour and hated that because of Rob's thoughtlessness, neither of us would be able to share in the biggest thing that had happened to either of us in our twenty-plus-year friendship.

We promised one another that we would have a sleepover with all the trimmings the minute I got back to New York the following month! She gave the phone to Rob and I did my best impression of humble and supportive best friend. (Maybe I was cut out for the movies!)

"Hey, could I get a beer?" I asked the bartender, amid a shower of the sounds so common at a crowded and very "open" bar.

"I'm sorry," the bartender said, "I didn't get that. What did you want?"

I leaned in, forgetting that I was wearing a strappy cream cami; the shrunken matching cardigan was long gone. I caught him peeking, harmlessly, and for whatever the reason, I didn't adjust a thing. "A beer!" I yelled.

"What kind?" he yelled back.

"Oh, I don't care, surprise me," I said as Victoria came over with another thirty-plus books that she wanted me to sign.

"Sweetcakes, I forgot these. Here," she said, handing me a

Sharpie. She tried telling me whom or what they were for but the music was too loud and there were people everywhere. I reached for the napkins, set up a makeshift tablecloth, and signed away. It was then that Victoria stepped on my foot and nudged me, and when I looked up at her she eyed the bartender. I followed her eyes but all I saw was him handing my nana a martini???

"What?" I mumbled, still signing.

"He's adorable," she cooed.

"Ya think?" I said, grabbing another glimpse.

"Man-opoly! And whew, does Mama want to play!"

"Mama's married," I reminded her.

"I know it," she said defeatedly. "But you're not."

"I'm not?" I sounded off sarcastically.

"Singlehood is wasted on the single!" she huffed, grabbed the books, and double-air-kissed me good-bye.

"You're out of here?" I asked.

"Yes. I'll talk to you tomorrow. And if he"—she tipped her head at the bartender—"is the reason you miss your flight, I'll be happy to find you another."

"Good-bye Boz-ley," I said, paying (almost) no mind to her quick comment. Just behind her were Daniel and May.

"Ciao," Victoria said and disappeared.

"How ya holding up?" May asked.

"I'm fine . . . This is kinda crazy, no?" I said, looking out onto the whole scene.

"I think it's awesome," Daniel proclaimed. "Hey, where's your drink?"

I realized that I had never been served. "Yeah, where is my drink?"

"Bartender!" May called. "Bartender!"

"Oh, May, hey look. There he is, babe," Daniel pointed out and May turned around excitedly, as did I. *There who is?* I thought.

HOLY MARY MOTHER OF . . .

"Nick, mate, hey man, thanks for coming," Daniel said and rough-hugged Nick, yes, Nick. My Nick. Well, not "my" Nick but well, whatever, I'll continue . . .

He didn't see me (yet) but I saw him and quickly turned to face the bartender, who was standing there with my beer ready to drop it on the bar. "Here ya—"

"Wait!" I said and grabbed the sleeve of his black button-down shirt. He looked a little frightened. "Oh, I'm sorry," I said, releasing his cotton. "I just, well, can I get a shot, no, a few shots, anything, quick. Please?"

"Sure," he smiled as I heard Nick and May getting acquainted.

"Viv," May said in a forced but casual way.

I pretended not to hear her.

"Viv."

Whistling, watching Victoria's bit of man-opoly.

"Vivian!" she barked, elbowing me in my back.

"Yes?" I said dropping my head to the floor, allowing my hair to cover my face à la Cousin It from *The Munsters*.

"Vivian?" she repeated questioningly.

"Yeah?" I said, now counting the cigarette butts on the floor.

"I want you to meet somebody . . . this is Nick, a friend of Daniel's from . . . from where again? I'm sorry."

To which Nick replied, "School."

"Right," May gushed apologetically. "Nick and Daniel took a few art classes together." When she saw that I wasn't really reacting, she went on, "Nick's also a tattoo artist . . . Vivian loves tattoos."

"Really?" he said.

There was a momentary silence and I was left with no choice. I looked up, brushed the hair from my face, and he said, "Hey." With a smile before I could utter a thing.

"Nice to meet you," he said, extending his hand.

Relieved, I said, "You, too." And we shook hands accordingly.

"So you're the author?" he remarked with tons of double en-tendre, in a way that only I could understand. Raising an eyebrow, he was playing with me, and I did my best to maintain my game face. I couldn't help but notice how good he looked. (Clothed.) Clean-shaven, black skinny blazer with a baby-blue-colored T-shirt underneath. "I guess a congratulations is in order." Again with that expressive eyebrow.

"Thank you," I said.

"Vivian!" the bartender shouted. "Your shots—"

"Shots?" May laughed.

"Sure!" I said. "Anyone?" I asked, as there just happened to be four sitting waiting to be digested. Together, we each did one, and it wasn't a few minutes before Nick and I were on our own.

"You look amazing."

"Thanks." I blushed. "You look pretty good yourself."

"Well, thanks. You never told me . . . about all of this."

"Yeah well . . ." I was at a loss for words. I had ruled out this kinda thing ever happening. And in a city as big as New York, where you barely ever even see your next-door neighbors, I'd thought that if I steered clear of that tattoo parlor, I basically would never have to face Nick again.

"So I gather you never told anyone about—"

"Shhh!" I pleaded, thoroughly paranoid. My eyebrows scrunched so hard I felt like I was scolding him rather than quieting him.

"Chill, girl. You think you're the only one at this bar who ever—"

"Take it easy," I interrupted him. "Not all of us are used to dealing with stuff like this."

"Really? I totally thought you . . . well, let's just say I would have never guessed."

I was immediately offended, and as much as I wanted a change of subject, that was no longer a possibility. "What are you saying, Nick? What could I have done or said to make you think that—"

"It's a compliment. Trust me."

"Oh really. I should be flattered that I come off easy!"

Now it was him with the "shhhhhh!" He put his pointer finger to my mouth and I caught May's mouth-drop. She and Daniel had returned. (Great!) "It was your confidence, that's all. That's what made me think . . . Aw, let's just forget it."

"Pardon me," my mom said. She had found me. "Vivian, honey, Daddy and I are going to go back to the hotel. Nana is, well, look . . ."

And there was my nana, fixing Drew's tie, whispering God only knows what in his ear. If it were anyone else I would have gone in and rescued him, but there was something devilishly pleasurable about the whole thing.

"We haven't met," she said while sizing up Nick.

This so wasn't happening . . .

"Nick. Nick Ryan. It's a pleasure." He smiled at my mom and firmly gripped my dad's hand. I was seconds from fainting.

Half looking at me and half looking at Nick, "Well, it's very nice to meet you, Nick. How do you all know each other?"

"Well, I'm a tattoo artist. I did Vivian—"

Emergency! Emergency! "He did my . . . site, Mom. We profiled Nick on my site."

"Oh. Okay then. How nice," she said.

"Let me walk you guys out, Ma. Nana looks . . . well, she looks tired." Drew was holding her hand, looking around for a family member no doubt.

"Yes, yes," she said and I ushered them out, respectfully giving Nick an *I-could-kill-you* look.

The party began to break up some forty minutes later. I had done about all the schmoozing I could. Every time I checked, and note that for some reason I was checking, Nick was watching me. And I was flattered in a pretty pathetic way. There was something a little "R" lurking about my normally "PG-13" existence. And I welcomed the upgrade!

I caught my brother chatting up an intern and beelined it over to the bar. I grabbed a seat next to Jayden, who looked like she was about to play a board game herself. "Hey you," I said, getting comfy.

"I'm crushing, Vivian," she confided, "big-time."

"You have my full support so long as he resides in New York," I joked.

"Very funny," she hissed. "Oh, hang on a second. I forgot to tell you, sorry very unprofessional, I just can't stop ordering drinks from him!" she laughed.

"It's fine," I assured her. "What's going on?"

"So Drew wanted me to tell you that they pushed back the big brouhaha meeting with the record label till the Tuesday after we get back. He said it was no big deal. That everything was moving ahead as planned. Something like that. We'll call him once we get settled out there."

"I'm so happy that you'll be with me, Jayden. It's going to be a lot of work but, trust me, we'll have a lot of fun!"

She was understandably distracted and didn't respond to my geeky-boring-teamwork babble.

"And another thing," she peeped.

"Yes?"

"Call me crazy because I did drink and I have only seen him in pictures, but I think Jack was here 'cause I could have sworn—"

I jumped off my bar stool. "What?"

"Jack-was-here," she pronounced. "I don't see him now, but he was here. I thought you knew."

"That's impossible," I said. "There's no way."

"Yeah, Vivian. He was right there," she said, pointing to the opposite corner of the bar. "Right over there."

I looked everywhere. Turned the bar inside out, went out back, checked downstairs, and even snuck into the men's room, but there was no sign of him. May and Daniel came over to say their good-byes and I stole her away for a minute.

"Jayden just said that she saw Jack here tonight. Did you?" I asked frantically.

"Really?" she teased.

"What do you mean really?"

"I sent him an invitation," she confessed.

"What!?! Why? Why didn't you tell me?"

"Because I was afraid that if he didn't show you would be disappointed. But who cares, because he did, right? Isn't that what counts?"

And over came Jayden. "Viv. Viv. There he is. There's Jack," she said excitedly.

"Where?" May and I said in tandem.

"There." Pointing to the sofa in the back of the space.

I looked while my heart skipped a beat but I couldn't be certain. The silhouette seemed familiar but other than that, I couldn't be sure. May and I held hands and crept closer. And then closer, and when Mr. X finally came into view, it wasn't Jack. Not even close.

"That's not Jack," May said.

"It's not?" Jayden replied innocently.

"You're fired," I said and May shook her head.

Not much later, May and Daniel skipped out. Then I made my final lap around and thanked everyone who'd come to support me. I had been waiting all night to pee and finally had the opportunity. When I emerged from the stall in the ladies' room, while washing my hands, my mind void of anything, I heard the door open and there was Nick. He closed and then locked it behind him. And he just stood there.

"It's great to see you again, Vivian," he said in a wolflike manner.

"Didn't we already cover that?" I said quickly, now updating my lipstick.

"Hey," he said pointedly, getting my attention. "Am I supposed to be sorry for that great night? 'Cause I'm not."

"That's just it, Nick. It was one great night." I put my lipstick back in my bag, trying to pretend like this was business as usual, and walked toward the door, hoping with all my might that he'd let me pass. "Let's not try to make it something it wasn't. Something that it's not."

"Yo," he said, placing himself right in front of me. "What's with this?" he asked, referring to my harsher-than-usual demeanor I guessed. "There's nothing wrong or bad going on here. Can't a guy be into you? Jesus."

"Yes. He can." I retreated to the sink and rested my bag on it. Nick was a good guy, despite the knuckles and the fact that he was skinnier than me. I could recognize that he wasn't going to bite or hassle me. I could tell that even with the designs he definitely had in his mind, he wanted to get a few thoughts across, too, and so I gave him the opportunity to do so.

"Look. I just want to get to know you better." He smiled crookedly.

I looked back at him questioningly.

"I do."

"Here," he added and walked toward me, not leaving much room between us. He reached inside his jacket pocket and removed a note of some sort. "I thought, hoped really, that you'd be the same Vivian when Daniel invited me here. I just had this strange feeling. So, I . . . made this for you."

"I don't know what to say."

"Don't say anything. It's no big thing."

I opened it, awkwardly. It was a homemade card with a sketch of Omelet on the front and a quick note of congratulations on the inside with roses scattered about.

"Thanks," I said. "You really didn't have to—"

He moved right in and finished my sentence with a kiss.

And there we were. After-hours in the ladies' room, making out for no apparent reason with only a freezing cold and very hard sink behind us. He didn't waste any time.

I pushed him away and said, "Listen. I like you. I do. Really. But this isn't comfortable for me. I feel like we don't have anywhere to go, since, well, since last time."

"We have everywhere to go," he said and pulled me into him.

"No," I said. "NO we don't."

"But Daniel said—"

"What?"

"That you were single."

"I am. But I'm not. I'm still in love with my ex-boyfriend and I'm not sure if he knows it and I just can't do this. I'm sorry. I just can't."

I grabbed my bag and kissed him on the cheek and left him in the ladies' room. I ran out of there much like Cinderella at eleven fifty-eight P.M. and stopped, amazed, at the sight of Jayden and the bartender, lip-locked by the DJ booth. *Good for her*, I thought.

Stephanie and a few other girls were still standing outside, holding their RSVP-slash-check-in lists while smoking and wrapping things up.

"Here," Stephanie said, handing me a packet of papers. "Victoria wanted you to look this list over when you have a chance. She said that you should send some thank-you notes to the VIPs who were here tonight."

"How am I supposed—"

"It's not that confusing." She grinned snidely. "Guests are listed alphabetically and then by association. Call Victoria if you want to, I'm going home." She flicked her cigarette, missing my toes by mere inches. Rather than dignify her attitude with a response, I elected instead to vamoose. Nick couldn't have been too far behind me and I didn't want to deal. Besides, I had already had my revenge knowing how much she'd undoubtedly detested checking in guests all night.

I lay awake with Omelet until my car came some four hours later to take me to the airport. I hated leaving him for so long when he hadn't been feeling so good. My brother, his uncle, would be taking care of him, and Joseph had every bit of care-for instructions and emergency contact information—a list longer than my legs—so I knew better than to worry. I just felt guilty, is all. I tried also to not let Jack's third brush-off sting but it did. How could it not? But, admittedly, it took a backseat to the rest of my evening. I made it.

I also knew I'd have to 'fess up to May about Nick at some point, but I actually looked forward to it—I've always been horrible at keeping secrets, especially my own. Besides, it had been ages since I'd done anything but complain about the men in my life. This confession would be juicy, and I for one was looking forward to a serious paradigm shift!

The weeks ahead were going to be the most exciting of my life. I didn't need a crystal ball to tell me that. I'd be venturing into cities I'd never been to before. Along with signings, I had radio spots and local television interviews scheduled. Once in Los Angeles, I'd be dealing with the optioning of my novel, too, and then I'd be back in time to wrap up my first record. Listen to me! It was all true but it felt so make-believe.

It was thrilling. These opportunities were just that: opportunities. But the fact that they even existed was enough of a nudge to keep me moving full steam ahead. Fears contained, with hope and spirit overflowing, I was poised to see them through . . .

twenty

By the time we got to Los Angeles, I had a newfound appreciation for the almost rich and barely famous. Touring was not, I repeat not, the glam-o-ramic experience I had imagined it would be. First-time authors are afforded less-than-luxurious everything. Coach fares, standard accommodations, and an incidentals budget that you had to monitor with a magnifying glass at all times. Our route was all over the place. Flying to one end of the country and then zigzagging about and back again. Over and over, and I ended up carrying that pungent airplane smell the entire month no matter how hard I scrubbed! We were in a constant MapQuest hell and just when we started to get to know a city, our schedule would quickly boot us out.

Beyond logistics and hotel bedding that would make you chafe, I got to know the little sister I never had, our Ms. Jayden, in a very new way. I found myself reminding her to remind me of all my whens and wheres and hows. Her directions would get us lost. Her remarks would get us in trouble. She was ripe and green and a wee bit too caught up in the idea of a "book tour" to settle down and be of any service to me. And that was just during the day. Nights were worse. I would wait up frantically if she stayed out late. I tried to turn the other cheek and ended up with a stiff neck, figure-eight style, as she was quite the sailor with a guy in almost every "port." (I still don't even know where she was meeting them!) She made me think twice about ever wanting a daughter of my own. The panic of it all . . . my poor parents!

I decided to set her free after our stint in Las Vegas. She had lost all of her money, the entirety of her checking and savings accounts. She woke me up hysterical at seven A.M. Having been up all night, she'd let it "ride" at the advice of a "friend" and, well, "poof" it was over. I consoled her as best I could, wrote her a check to cash when she got back to New York, bought her a one-way ticket home, and sent her packing. Los Angeles was going to be crazy enough; I couldn't deal with another soap opera.

The strange part of all this was twofold. First, I missed the little bugger the minute she left, and second, I couldn't really ever say that I was angry with her. I was annoyed, in a big big way, but not mad. I loved that she was wild and all over the place. She reminded me, often, of who I, until recently, had been and why I had gotten as far as I had in the first place: She was so open. Open to new experiences. Open to mischief and love and laughter. She was my ambition personified: to stay real amid the madness. I'd hoped she'd rub off on me as the chaos and pressures mounted.

But she hadn't. She backfired. Her energy deflected off me instead of on, making me feel old and stiff and serious. The responsible thing was to find a balance. Have fun while I went through the motions. That was what I was aiming to do.

But that was easier said than done. Sans Jayden, I was still getting lost, was arriving late, and didn't have anyone to freak out with. But I made it through with only a few serious wounds and wrapped my first book tour somewhat successfully.

With my luggage waiting patiently in the back of my car, I was parked out front of LAX waiting for Sheryl's plane to arrive. She would be joining me for the very last leg of my trip and thankfully uprooting me from my sulfuric stay at the lodge du jour on the outskirts of Hollywood. The plan was that she and I would be staying with Jacquelyn and fam in what was billed as "paradise," their beachfront condo à la Marina del Rey, while we shopped production companies for my book.

I couldn't have been more excited to see her. Only hours before—lonely as all hell, broke as could be (having cleaned out my savings account helping Jayden refill hers), straightening my hair with an iron that she had accidentally left behind in the bathroom of this domestic dis of a hotel room—I'd been inexplicably brought to tears. I had had the television on in the distance, listening to *The Price Is Right* because silence, at this juncture, was just way too depressing, and when the game show's theme music started up and the announcer Rod Roddy told some poor out-of-towner to "Come on down! 'Cause you're the next contestant on *The Price Is Right*!" something triggered within me and I just lost it. I dropped the straightening iron on the filmy bathroom floor, petrified of missing a single beat of the show, and sat atop my rock-hard bounceless bed and was overcome with joy for the stranger I saw skipping down an aisle and taking her place among a handful of people, ready to play her heart out for a boring set of grayish-white kitchen dishes.

When I caught a glimpse of my reflection on the telly, blubbering, with my hair parted down the middle dramatically dividing kinky curls from the satined-out straight ones and desperately hoping that my girl from Boise, Idaho, would go the distance, win her dishes, make it to that archaic wheel, spin her heart out, get to the final round, and take it all that I knew it was time to check out, immediately!

So I threw my stuff into my bag, sat on it and bounced up and down till I managed to get it shut, and then made my way to the airport. I got there (very) early, only to discover that Sheryl's plane was running (very) late. After I'd already tweezed my eyebrows, bitten off my nails, sipped my third cup of coffee, cleaned out the glove compartment, and listened to about all the (same) music I could take, I had the brilliant idea of unpacking and repacking my suit-case in an effort to pass the time.

All of my favorites (tops, jeans, dresses) had been worn so many times that I could barely stand the sight of them anymore. I was so over living out of a bag and anxiously anticipated the day when, home, I would open my closet and bask in the options! I was further perturbed by the newsprint that had apparently stained my trea-sured white jeans. I had been saving the local newspapers that re-viewed my book or did a story on me, keeping clippings for a scrapbook, for Sheryl, for my mom, whoever cared. So all this time I was sure I'd been placing them in the secret side compartment of my suitcase . . . I hadn't. Instead I'd been sandwiching them with my clothes. And in this instance and with my good luck, next to my tight-ee white-ees. Brilliant! Argh.

Now cruelly reminded of what went where, I unzipped the side compartment of my bag and gently began to place my press clip-pings within. Not so fast. There was something else in this same place that was getting in my way. So I reached inside and felt an enve-lope, pulled it out, and opened it up. And there was the marked-up guest list—which I had completely spaced on—from my after-party, now three-plus weeks past.

Under normal circumstances I would have been aggravated with myself for forgetting to send the thank-yous that Victoria had wanted, but with more than an hour to kill waiting for Sheryl, this was the best busywork I had ever come in contact with.

Bag repacked and notes out front, I amused myself with this sudden project. I put a face to every name and made careful men-tal notes of my no-shows. I went down the list, noting the notables and, using the hotel stationery I'd "borrowed," did what the boss had asked. With a severe hand cramp forty-five minutes in, Sheryl called on my cell phone. Her plane had just landed.

"I'm here!" she announced happily.

"Thank God!" I said. "How was your flight?"

"Nightmare," she proclaimed. "Total nightmare!"

"Aw, Sher—"

"My vegetarian meal went missing, a toddler behind me had an ear infection, and I had already seen the in-flight movie—twice!"

"Well, it's all over now," I comforted.

"I know! I can't wait. This is going to be awesome!"

"I know it!" I yelped.

"I'll meet you out front. Gate . . . thirty-four," she said.

"Like, when, twenty minutes? Baggage claim is going to be from hell."

"Ha ha ha." She laughed me off. "Who do you think you're dealing with? [Pause] It's so about the carry-on!"

Leave it to Sheryl.

We hung up and I pulled around as instructed. I began to collect my thank-yous and took one last quick glimpse at the list. I was on T and so felt like finishing. No one to thank in U, I thought, and no one to thank in—WAIT!

JACK VICTOR, the line read . . . checked.

He had been there. Jayden was right.

Knock. Knock. Knock.

Knock. Knock. Knock.

Pound. Pound. Pound.

". . . e-e-n?!?"

". . . e-e-n?!?"

There was Sheryl flailing her arms in front of my car. As if she were standing in front of a moving vehicle begging it to stop.

I pressed UNLOCK and she opened the door. "Girlfriend! The radio's not even on??? You didn't hear my tapping?"

She looked me over, trying to figure out what was happening. With a blink of an eye she grabbed the guest list to see what had distracted me. I watched her as she read each name. I counted down silently in my head, timing her, knowing she'd figure it out eventually.

Five . . .

Four . . .

Three . . .

Two . . .

"Noooooooooo," she yelled silently.

I nodded my head yes, put the key in the ignition, and pressed my foot against the gas.

"Screw Marina del Rey," she said, "I know a great bar on Melrose."

twenty-one

T he thirty-plus-minute ride from LAX to Hollywood was a quiet one. At least for me. While I slumped silently behind the wheel, Sheryl was busy utilizing modern-day technology—her virtual office on the road. Between voice mail and some random handheld device that enabled her to get online and comb through e-mails, she had her A.D.D.-laden hands full. Which was, actually, a blessing in disguise, as I fully needed to obsess over the details of my personal life before I could actually articulate any of them.

"Right over here," she directed. "Vivian, right here!"

"But this is Venice?" I said while trying to not cause a major traffic accident, steering off Pacific Avenue in negative time.

"No? Really?" she quipped. "Jacks said she saw Brad Pitt here last weekend!"

The "here" Sheryl was referring to was a restaurant-slash-bar called The Canal Club.

"It's only a few minutes from Jacks's place and truth be told, I'm starved. It's another twenty to anywhere Melrose. And if the food's good enough for Brad, then, well, hey, I'm sure it will be good enough for me."

I couldn't argue that rationale and flicked my keys at the valet. With early evening looming, the darkening sky reflected my spirit. I still couldn't get my head around the fact that I had missed Jack.

We entered The Canal Club, the perfect L.A. version of a pan-Asian hideaway. Crowded enough that everyone minded their own business but still early enough that a choice table could be found. Sheryl canvassed the menu as I destroyed a pretty paper umbrella that I ripped from the bar. "What are you going to have?" she asked.

"I'm not that hungry."

"C'mon, Vivian—order something," she said.

"What can I get you guys?" a handsome waiter (definitely actor) questioned. "Happy-hour sushi is still in effect, in case you're interested."

A sushi pro, Sheryl ordered impressively. I, on the other hand, caught a glimpse of a big fat brownie (*fat* being the operative word) topped with vanilla ice cream and a glowing candle perched above.

"That," I said, pointing.

"With or without a candle?" he joked.

"Without," I grinned.

"Good for you," Sheryl supported. "Good-for-you."

"Thanks." I smiled.

"So what is this?" She was referring to my less-than-happy persona. "Please tell me I didn't fly across the country to be brought down by you? Did you, even for a second, look on the bright side, Vivian? Hello? He was there!!!"

"I know, you're right, I should be psyched about that. But it's just the karma that's getting to me. I mean, really, why is this all so difficult? And still, Sher, who knows what's going to happen, you know? He could tell me that he's not interested."

"Yeah, right, and I could tell you that the moon is made of cheese. [Pause.] Hey, and speaking of, do you smell pizza?"

"Oh my God, you're ravenous! Hey!" I shouted to cute waiter boy. "Please, please, please get this lady some bread!"

"Listen, V. We need to finish the Jack conversation here and now—"

"Hope this will do," said the cute waiter boy, dropping some fancy veggie pan-Asian doohickey on our table.

"Is that even edible?" I asked. It looked like a weed pulled from a fancy garden. Before I could answer she chimed, "Ignore my friend, please, she's just bitter because we didn't go to In-N-Out Burger."

"Very clever, Sher," I said.

"Sure," she agreed. "But true." She took a nibble of the weed in question and spit it immediately into her napkin.

I smiled, all knowingly.

"Back to matters of the heart," she insisted. "It's so important that you put your best foot forward this week. You need to shelve your love life for one more week and when you get back, like the minute you get back, you need to call him, lay it all out on the line, and . . . then live happily ever after."

I grunted, as if it could ever be that easy.

"I'm serious!" she said. "What good is it going to do you to focus on what might have been, what could have been, why you didn't see him. Why he didn't approach you. It's past. It's over. You're in L.A. with me trying to option your book. I mean, c'mon now: Does this kind of shit ever happen in real life?"

"No," I murmured.

"Exactly. People dream of this kind of stuff. They see it in movies. They read it in books. I mean, you're living it out right here, right now. Get over yourself and be psyched!!!"

"You're right," I conceded. "As usual."

"Exactly." She grinned. "Exactly."

The "V" Spot

Our food came and she hovered over her meal like a very happy vulture.

"Honestly," she said, "I need a raise. You artists . . . always with the drama!"

As I spooned myself silly with the richest, most delicious dessert I think I've ever had the pleasure of devouring, I gave a second thought to Sheryl's pearls of wisdom. She was dead-on. I needed to get it together already; this was just way too incredible to tarnish with anything in the *amoré* department.

She proceeded to explain the week's worth of appointments and meetings we had, and, again, covered the ways of the world here in la-la land. Our mission would be multilayered. Not only did I need to find a production company that would agree to pay for and make my novel into a television show or film, but I then needed to find a distributor—a network or otherwise—that would agree to air it. I would leave the negotiating up to Sheryl and Jacks and Stan and the lawyers. It was my job to dance.

Bellies full, we waited outside for the valet to retrieve our car.

"How's your man, Sher?" I asked. "I feel so bad. I've been so wrapped up in all of this. I'm sorry. Tell me."

"What's to tell" she sighed. "He's, he's . . ."

"Yeah?"

"He's wonderful," she purred, staring at her bejeweled ring finger.

"Good for you, Sher. I'm so happy for you!"

"Are you really?" she questioned.

"Of course I am!" I answered defensively.

Getting into the car, she explained, "Sure you are. Of course you are."

"Of course I am."

"I just remember when my roommate, former roommate, had called it quits with her man, and I was so relieved. Sure, it was a self-ish emotion, but it was my instinctual emotion just the same. It was rough, being the only single girl for what felt like miles and miles."

"I hear you," I said, locking my seat belt and driving off, "and that's mighty honest of you to say. But I've been the lone single ranger for almost a year now. I've grown very used to it." *God, has my world changed,* I thought.

"Gotcha." She got Jacquelyn on the phone. "Jacks?" she yelped. "We're here! Like five minutes away."

She got what I assumed was the balance of our directions and mouthed and/or pointed them on to me. In less than five minutes we were there. It was dark so I couldn't see the ocean, but I could fully hear and smell it. It was like popping a pill: The moment we were out of the car, I felt like a whole new person. So chill. I was happy to have Sheryl by my side despite her sometimes brutal way of expressing herself. Could she have been on to something, when speaking of my possible disappointment regarding her glowing love life?

Nahhhh. I didn't think so.

Jacks greeted us outside the gates to her parking garage. She looked like she could be Goldie Hawn's oldest daughter, Sophie's long-lost sister. (Think eight years and eighteen pounds on Kate Hudson.) Baby in tow, she was wearing a pair of old tattered Levi's tucked into Nanook-of-the-North-ish caramel-colored ski boots. (This was my very first UGG sighting, so forgive my fashion faux pas.) She had a heather-gray tank top underneath a cream-colored fisherman sweater; the tie along the waist was undone, and the baby had one end in her mouth while the other dragged, nearly, along the ground.

"Look at you!" Sheryl cried, dropping her suitcase on my foot.

"Look at you, Shoe-Shoe!" Jacks screamed back. Handing her baby off to me??!??!!?

With a bag paper-weighting me to the gravel and a baby now sticking a few wet fingers in my ear I could only smile awkwardly, not sure if I wanted to cry, laugh, or whine, *Ewwwwwwwww!*

As they hugged and smooched and gallivanted about in an almost sisterly way, it felt as if they had forgotten about me, er, us, entirely. "Ahem," I noted. "Ahem."

"So you must be Vivian?" she greeted.

"Yup," I confirmed. "And this is—?" I handed her back her child.

"Dorothy. We call her D for short."

"Hey D!" Sheryl laughed. Picking her up from her mother. Holding her just above her face. "Hey D! Hey little D D D!"

And with that D puked, hitting Sheryl's chin and making it down her neck and blouse.

And then I was shocked. Sheryl, our Sheryl, didn't bat an eye.

"Oh my, Sher—I'm so sorry!!!" Jacks scrambled, searching for words as well as for something to wipe her down with all at the same time. "She just finished her dinner."

"Don't worry about it, Jacks," Sheryl insisted.

"What are we still doing out here?" Jacquelyn questioned as she tried to wipe Sheryl up with the wrap to her sweater. "Let's go inside."

We took a small elevator to the third of three floors. When the door opened I could not believe my eyes: We were looking at a floor-to-ceiling view, panorama style, of the moonlight as it reflected off the ocean with every navy to purple to pink shade you could think of.

"Holy shit!" I said accidentally as they both started to laugh.

"Pretty amazing, right?" Sheryl said.

"Jacquelyn—this is magnificent," I continued.

"I know. I know. It makes leaving, doing anything productive really, almost impossible."

Allow me to explain. Jacquelyn's home was on the beach. Not near or beside or anything like that. It was right smack on it. So there weren't any walls or anything obstructing the view of the ocean. And what they did was have every room face the ocean, looking out an enormous window. It was like "wallpaper," if you will, the beach and the ocean. Always changing, colors, atmospheres, sights from day to night. It was incredible and quite distracting for the first little bit.

Soon her husband and toddleresque son came home. After the

parents, together, put the babies down to bed, we four went to sip tea on their balcony and map out our plan.

I was quickly taken aback by their generosity and immediate affection for me and my mission. It was as if they wanted me (and Sheryl) to succeed as much as they would themselves. It was a very us-against-the-world type of fire-drill-slash-conversation. I was both lectured and forewarned about what was to take place and whom we would be meeting with.

"Keep everything very simple," Samuel, Jacks's husband, advised. "These people have a very short attention span and even less patience. They make up their minds almost before you finish your first sentence."

"Lovely," I mumbled.

"They take meetings like yours," Jacks added, "all day long. Imagine, they're listening to pitches, some great, some not, by schooled pros and by newbies, day in and day out. So just keep that in mind."

"But this is different," Samuel figured. "She's real, you know"—he was looking at me, speaking to Sheryl and Jacks as if I weren't even there. "She's lived it, she wrote it, the site's real, people love it. She's got one up on everyone with an idea already."

"So true," Sheryl concurred.

"Totally," Jacks said and grabbed my hand underneath the cast-iron table. "He's so right!"

Samuel broke out a listing complete with addresses and telephone numbers of our meetings. The first were with studios that anyone would recognize. Names and logos we've all seen and heard for years and years. Which made my stomach turn and turn and turn.

"Remember," he said as he scooped up our mugs and leftover tea bags, walking back inside toward the kitchen, "no matter what, it's their job to find talent like you so, even though this is a long shot in many ways, in many ways it's not!"

"I so love him!" Sheryl pointed out to Jacks.

"I know." She glowed. "I do, too!"

I went to bed that night with the help of my childhood sleepy-time antidote that was appropriate then, when popping sleeping pills would have been unheard of: I counted back slowly from one hundred with my eyes closed. I breathed and breathed and told myself that the sooner I fell asleep, the sooner I would get to begin this adventure. The longer I struggled with it and kept myself up, the worse it would all be. So I began counting back and thought of Jack and coming back to New York a "winner."

Looking back, I wish I'd realized that I had won already. Wish I'd been able to swallow the kind of pill that allows you to see your accomplishments regardless of what happens next.

That's the true sign of a winner.

twenty-two

I spent the next three months in California. Within the first two weeks I'd signed with a manager and an agent, a week after that I won a production deal, and a week later I sold a script to a major network.

Crowning Productions put me up at Shutters on the Beach in Santa Monica. Although there was something safe and sweet about staying with Jacquelyn and fam, at the same time there was a tinge of something a little inappropriate, too. (It had nothing to do with becoming schooled in the world of diapers via Dorothy—a trade that I've been assured will come in handy many moons from now in my own lifetime.) I just felt like I had outstayed my welcome, is all. Jacks will deny this to this day. She even offered to stay at Shutters for me while I minded her two children and fed her gentle husband when I gave her my departure date. So, after a cool stay in Marina del Rey, I checked into Shutters, the luxe hotel to end all luxe hotels. Moreover, even my rental car was upgraded to a silver Saab convertible—and, get this, every expense you could imagine was miraculously covered by the studio. Had I woken up one morning a size six, it would have been proof positive that this was all a saccharine-filled dream.

I was told that I had gotten farther than most, here in la-la land: the efficient and affectionate trusted manager, the big-time hard-core get-it-done agent, the coveted proactive production com-pany, the hungry open-minded network. But in my mind it all just flowed. It all felt right, serendipitous. But not without tons of grueling work. Wrapped, definitely, in happy bright adorable meant-to-be paper.

Never had I sweat so much. No treadmill or cardio class will ever come close. Never had I expelled so much emotional energy in meeting after meeting postured with friendly faces and open arms. Never had I dealt with the constant dry mouth that only an over-the-counter drug sidelines you with. And I'd never spent so much time, collectively, in a bathroom. Getting my (first) TV deal made writing the first book feel like a bike ride. As a rookie, I could only imagine what people in the entertainment industry went through, season in and season out, trying to go all the way. It's a mind game that doesn't come with a set of directions, where the highs are Everest-like and the lows, well, they're just plain cruel.

After negotiating every inch, every if and when of my contracts complete with syndication, credit, and salary, anyone would have thought that this was going to go "all the way." That come fall, I'd have a show on the air in some way, shape, or form.

During those three months, I'd wake up every morning and take a shower in the most amazing bathroom that, in my opinion, had ever been built. I'd sip cappuccino, crunch on buttered whole wheat toast, all escorted to my room by a uniform-clad pleasure-ized member of the wait staff, and I'd read the morning papers in the most divine white terry bathrobe all on the terrace of my pimped-out room. Which, I'll have you know, situated me right above the ocean. I felt like a modern-day Marilyn Monroe or some-thing. Come ten A.M., my fax, also in my room, would go into overdrive, spitting out sheets consisting of work from New York, agreements from L.A., scribbled notes from friends. And being three hours behind NYC on West Coast time, the moment I pressed SEND/ RECEIVE on my laptop, well, it was dizzying.

But hey, who in their right mind would or could ever complain? Being frantically busy under the Shutters roof and care ain't exactly the worst thing in the world.

Even better, while working the television angle in Los Angeles, most of my day-to-day responsibilities in New York were being covered by May and Jayden. Which meant I could sit down at sunset every night, again on my terrace, and bang out what would become my second novel.

If you think that somewhere in all this, I had forgotten about Jack, you're wrong. I thought about him more than ever. Only instead of putting myself through regret-laden torture, I thought about all our good times, how proud he would be of me, and how much we had to look forward to in our future. I had always believed that I needed to do something and be someone before I settled down, and now with a pack of mighty men and women behind me all telling me how great I was, how special, how successful I'd be, well, that was all the assurance I needed to finally believe in myself. (Lame but true.)

Disguised beneath hope and dreams, signals and steps, unbeknownst to me I was really just another tragic cliché, another princess of the "almost," and even with my head screwed on as tight as humanly possible, trying admirably not to believe all the hype and keep it as real as possible, well, at the end of the day, with all the props, all the triggers clicking and going off around me, I couldn't help but believe that everything that I was being positioned for was eventually going to be realized.

If you've read this far in my book—or if this is the second book of mine that you've read, or even the third—you'll know that I am a very theatrical person. Not in front of the camera but behind my persona. I live my life in an almost third-party dream sequence. I'll try to explain: Nearly every major experience in my own life or every major emotional moment I've had seems to bring me back to some moment in a favorite film, a favorite show, or a favorite story. And because I am one of those girls who can't get enough romantic comedies, where the imperfect leading lady makes it happen for herself, well, you can only imagine how true to life these three months were. Without a relative or close friend in the biz, I could only draw from my make-believe ones. The experiences and emotions of my favorite heroines were strikingly similar to those that I was having myself. And it felt real 'cause it was real—but it wasn't all at the same time. My life, those months, was jarring. And like most of you, 'cause it's only natural, I am a sucker for happy endings. What woman isn't? And of course our heroines always seem to get it together before the theme music and credits appear. So judging by what I knew to be true and real—albeit pop fiction—I would have bet my last dollar on a "happily ever after" of my very own.

I remember, quite vividly and even more fondly, driving up to the security gates at Crowning Productions, a vast studio that was bigger than two high schools and three strip malls combined in my hometown. Then pulling into a designated parking space, trying to make out the faces around me I knew were famous behind dark sunglasses. Being greeted by producers all ready and eager to talk shop, where shop included my ideas, my take, my thoughts on my show. Meeting talented accomplished writers and such, all just as excited to meet me and work on something fresh and different—my show.

I also remember how the hair on my arms would stick up straight when I would relay a day in the life of me, either in my convertible or on my terrace, to my proud parents, my giggly friends, knowing that if the situation were reversed I'd be convinced they were putting me on, exaggerating at the very least. And because I knew I wasn't, because I knew that I was being thoroughly honest in every which way, well, it was just too good to be true.

Literally.

But we'll get there in a few.

Adding flames to the *you've-got-to-be-kidding-me* fire was the record I had been working on simultaneously. With twelve songs approved and licensed, my first album was well on its way to being complete. We had been awaiting the go-ahead on one final song for the compilation: "Heartbreaker" by Pat Benatar. It was so important to me that we get this song on the album because I think it's the best song ever from a woman to a man who has wreaked havoc with her heart. It's not sad and sappy, it's angry. And that is very, very hard to find. I also dug the fact that it's an eighties song and thought that, for younger listeners, it would be something fresh, while for those of us who are old enough to remember, it would be a bit of salty nostalgia.

Long story short, however, we were not able to snag it from her. Reasons that I can't really get into. That said, leave it to May to come up with a Plan B. One that I loved her for then hated her for and thanked her for all in a week's time.

Read on . . .

twenty-three

I had just received some disturbing news from Joseph: Omelet, apparently, still wasn't feeling so hot. "Not to worry," he assured me. "Maybe I'll just have to drive him cross-country so that he can see his mama, and so I can get myself one of those cute actresses. Ha ha ha."

"What do you mean, Joseph?" I worried.

"You know, a hottie."

"No! Of course I knew what you meant! I mean Omelet. Have you taken him back to the vet?"

"Yes. And Mom and Dad came in last weekend and we all spoiled him rotten and he's fine. Don't worry."

"Promise?"

"Promise. Just get your show on the air. I need a hottie."

Uch.

I thought about how my brother really was one of "those guys." The guys that me and my friends spend hours agonizing over, dissecting, looking for that glimmer of maturity . . . and, well, if that noncommittal-creep gene runs in your own family, what does that say about the rest of the male population???

My next call came in as I was slurping down a mocha ice blended from Coffee Bean & Tea Leaf on Montana. I was trying to open the car door, find my cell phone, and not spill my drink, and, never the juggler, dropped the latter, decorating the pavement with my six-dollar refreshment.

Bugger!

"Hello," I grunted.

"Vivian. It's Drew."

"And May," May said.

"And Sheryl," Sheryl said.

"And Stan," Stan said.

"And Daniel," Daniel said.

Drew again: "We're all here, conference room. May had an idea . . ."

"Hang on, hang on . . . ," I pleaded, getting situated, finding the lighter to recharge my dying phone, the ignition to activate it, and the volume on my radio, to lower it—severely!

"What's up?" I questioned, signaling that I was ready.

"May, why don't you start?" Stan suggested.

"Hey V," she said.

"Hi May. So . . . tell me."

"Okay," she started. "So I knew how much you wanted 'Heart-breaker,' and since Pat's reps aren't budging, I thought about doing a cover of it?"

"A cover?" I asked innocently.

"A cover track," Sheryl blurted impatiently.

"Oh, like have another band sing it," I said. "Very cool idea, May!"

She hesitated. "Well, kind of."

"What do you mean, *kind of*?"

"Well, Drew and I sat down with the label and we went through a whole list of singers who could maybe do it—"

"Yeah."

"And well, either this one was on tour, or that one was in rehab, blah, blah, blah."

Drew, excitedly: "So May had this brilliant idea!"

"What?" I asked eagerly.

To which May replied: "Well, I sort of threw it out there, that, well, that, um, that maybe you should do it."

"Do what?" I asked. I had no idea what she meant.

"That you should sing it," Stan said.

"What?" I chuckled. "You're kidding me right? I mean, there's no way."

"Why's that again?" Sheryl prompted.

"Why? Well, for starters, I can't sing."

"That never stopped J. Lo," Daniel joked.

"Ha. Ha," I said.

"Or Britney," Drew offered.

"Or Madonna, for that matter," said May.

"Okay, that's going too far," I said, defending the Material Girl.

After a brief silence, Stan threw his weight around. "We just want you to give it a try, Vivian, that's all we're saying."

"Asking, right? You meant asking?"

"Um. NO. I'm afraid not, Vivian," he bellowed.

To which Sheryl informed me, "We booked studio time for you tomorrow."

"Have you all gone mad?" I laughed. "This is absurd."

"Absurd as you selling a script to Crowning Productions?" Drew pointed out.

"I know where you're going with this, Drew. And I appreciate the vote of confidence. But I mean, c'mon now. Have you all forgotten last year's Christmas party and the karaoke machine?"

Silence.

"May, back me up here . . . please!" I begged.

"That's the whole point, V," she explained. "It would be a goof . . . only a good goof."

"We're not expecting you to become a recording artist. It's a fun thing and a way for you to get the song on the record," Drew said.

"Tell her about the band," Daniel urged.

"What? Now there's a band. You guys are killing me here."

"There's not a band, Vivian," Drew pacified me. "I have a few friends who play music in Chicago—"

"An orchestra?"

"No." He laughed. "They're a band, a great band, but it's not like they're going to be your band. I just asked them to lay down the track for us. Take the eighties out and make it edgy, make it now."

"Listen to you!" I teased. "You've been spending too much time on this, Drew!"

"Sure, laugh it off now," he said. "But later, when it works, when it's kick-ass, you'll be thanking me."

"You're dreaming," I snorted.

"Knock it off," Stan interjected. "I have a lunch meeting. Sheryl, just make sure she knows where to go and when. Get her the lyrics and . . . and get on a plane. Tonight. I don't want a phone call in the morning that she forgot or got lost or chickened out."

I was as excited as I was petrified as I was pissed that Stan was barking at my friends and talking about me as if I weren't even there. The fact that I didn't respond made my feelings apparent.

"We'll call you later," Drew peeped and hung up before things got hostile.

Then it hit me. Sheryl had said *tomorrow* . . .

twenty-four

Before you could sing "Your love is like a tidal wave," lyrics to "Heartbreaker" were faxed to my room at Shutters and her CD *Pat Benatar: The Collection* was waiting with the concierge.

I'm serious.

There it was, waiting, staring straight at me. I decided to take another shower (yes, it's pretty startling how clean you can be when you love your bathroom) and put the CD on, just as a little experiment.

Well, normally when you sing in the shower, you're at your best: You know no one is listening, you're basically unaware that you're even in full singing mode, and, well, it's just mindless and fun. But it's a completely new thing when it's no longer in the back but rather in the forefront of your mind, resting there—the notion of having to sing it for real. And just as I was (deep) conditioning, "Heartbreaker" surfaced and I went with it, until, well, until I realized that this was just ludicrous.

(Next time you hear "Heartbreaker," really listen to it. Pat's range is ridiculous, the vocals are intense, and it's fast as hell!)

I was, pardon my word choice but it is, simply, apropos . . . fucked!

I stepped out of the shower and tried it again.

Nope.

And again.

Nope.

And again.

Nothing.

Houston, we have a problem.

I hit SPEAKER and dialed Drew.

"This is Drew."

"This is Pat," I said flatly.

He laughed.

I laughed.

And then I freaked. "I can't do it!" I shrieked. "I can't! There's just no way, Drew!"

"Calm down!" he urged.

"Calm down?" I yelped. "I can't calm down. Sheryl's on a plane. It's all set. And it's tomorrow Drew. I mean, c'mon, tomorrow?"

"Vivian, relax."

"No!" I stomped.

"Viviannnn," he implored. "You've said *I can't* more in this one conversation than I think I've heard you say it in what, almost three years."

"Yeah I know. But lose the pep talk 'cause it ain't gonna work this time, Drew!"

"You are taking this way too seriously."

"Oh really?"

"Uh-huh."

"I'm just a guinea pig to you. To all of you!"

"Is that so?"

"Yup. You guys just throw me into these situations with no regard—"

He interrupted me. "With no regard? That's crap. What any of us wouldn't do for these experiences. You really need to think about that."

"Uh-huh—"

"Seriously, Vivian. If it sucks we'll bag it and no one will have to know we even tried."

"Good try," I said. "Like the whole office and the entire label doesn't know that you've already put me up to this?"

"Think about it this way, will you—"

"I'm listening—"

"You know what I wouldn't give to step in for Bruce—" That would be Springsteen. Drew worshipped him. "—even just for a second. Just to know what that feels like."

"But," I tried.

"No buts, Vivian. Just try. That's all I'm, any of us, are asking. Just give it a try."

"Uch, fine," I said reluctantly.

"Go in there tomorrow expecting it to suck and maybe you'll be pleasantly surprised," he advised.

"Maybe not," I mumbled.

"It's great fodder for the books."

"It's called fiction, Drew. Ever heard of it? I am at liberty to make stuff up. I don't have to actually live what I write," I informed him.

"I know. So then make yourself sound like Mariah Carey. Just use it 'cause it's such a 'Vivian' thing. This opportunity doesn't happen to many mortals."

"You should have quit while you were ahead," I noted.

"Just shut up and do it."

"Right."

"And get back here already. This place isn't the same without you."

I laughed. "Good-bye," I said.

"Later." He checked out.

I put the song on again and tried to be serious. At least, I thought, I knew the words already; that part would be easy. But try as I might it just wasn't flowing. And that's putting it mildly.

I ordered up a Caesar salad, put my queen-for-a-day robe back on, and brought my cell phone outside. I looked out my balcony and let Drew's comments marinate.

He was right. About all of it. Sure there was a little Britney in me just dying to get out. Once. One time. I wasn't delusional. Even I knew my limits. NO crazy career goals lurking to walk on to the *TRL* set one day. This would be a goof, a lark, and another unbelievable story I could tell my grandchildren one day. Even if they did end up to be doggies.

I phoned Sophie and was disappointed to get her voice mail. Last we spoke, she'd been looking at venues for her wedding, without me. I made her swear that she would hold out on any dress shopping till I got back. Flowers and bands and food I didn't care about. But wedding dresses, that was my jurisdiction! I sighed and tried Sheryl, but she was long gone. May didn't answer her phone but I guessed that that was intentional. And then I tried Jack. With the rest of my boundaries thoroughly broken down, I didn't think about the possible casualties of such a call. Instead, in my mind, I made as if talking and trading calls was the norm. I missed him so and wanted to hear his voice.

But his number had been disconnected.

I tried once more, thinking that perhaps I'd misdialed, but again, *"The number you have reached, blah, blah, blah."*

I thought little of it. Maybe he forgot to pay his bill. Maybe he changed it. I'd try again, at his work, the next day, or the day after that. When the inclination surfaced.

I sat up all night singing my heart out, tearing my voice to that of Demi Moore with a chest cold. Until, that is, I got an awkward phone call from the front desk. Apparently he'd been receiving complaints from other guests.

Genius!

twenty-five

I was sure I'd staged a wake-up call for nine A.M.; having not fallen asleep until dawn, I thought it satisfactory. But when there was a knock at my door and a voice that announced, "Room service," I stumbled up, glancing at my alarm clock, which boldly said that it was barely eight. I was revved up and ready to give anyone who was listening a piece of my fried mind.

But when I opened the door and saw Sheryl in a scant chino flight suit and Timberland-inspired Manolos, I thought perhaps I was caught somewhere between a Beyoncé Knowles video and a naughty nightmare!

"Good morning, rock star!" Sheryl declared, prancing right past me, cooing, "How exciting is this?!?" She proceeded to snap my picture with the digital camera hidden in her savvy cell phone before I'd even opened my second eye.

I fumbled back into my bed, mumbling like an old man, and covered myself with the sloppy manhandled thousand-thread-count bed linens.

Sheryl explored my room, opened every blind, turned on the

television, and managed to get room service on the phone in ten seconds flat.

She jumped on my bed, tore off my covers, and shoved me till I sat up.

"I cannot believe this setup!" she cried, astonished.

Stretching, I replied, "I know."

"We've got two hours and I think we should leave in about thirty minutes. You know: L.A. traffic."

Knowing she would never yield, I got up, removed my wedgie, trying as hard as possible to ignore her, and plopped myself into the shower. It was minutes before I heard "Heartbreaker" coming from outside. I quickly steeled myself for what was about to take place.

"Sing it for me, Viv!" Sheryl begged on our way to what would be my first and absolute last recording session.

"Not on your life," I said bitterly.

"Plllllllleeeeeaaaasssse!"

I ignored her still, turning up the radio, again with the silent treatment. I wasn't angry; I don't want to give that impression. I was just a nervous wreck. Divided between complete fear and unadulterated manic excitement. This was the most undone I had ever remembered being. The fact that I was (somewhat) able to control my bodily functions came as a complete and very welcome surprise. I sing in the privacy of my own space. I can't even get into it when I know *Omelet* is listening. I only karaoke on special occasions while under the influence, knowing full well that I won't recollect a single sour note come sunrise!!!

We pulled up to a nearly vacant studio outside Burbank—only three cars inhabited the vast parking lot. Sheryl entered first, the squeak of the door still present in my mind even as I type. The place was dark, I was sure, unless I was seconds from blacking out. It was only when Sheryl hollered "Hello?" and a lone voice yonder replied, "Yo! We're back here" that I knew my fate was sealed.

Three guys, all ragged in a purposeful way, stood to greet us while pointing their cigarettes downward so as not to offend. With marked-up T-shirts that looked like they had been slept in, baggy jeans held up by some backward version of gravity, shiny white sneakers, a solid amount of bling-bling, two shaved heads and one hairy how-do-you-do, capped and tilted sideways, they each had the makings of every stereotypical producer ever seen on cable TV.

Rog—not Roger—was the mouthpiece of the lot, explaining that we had five hours, which, he assumed, would be more than enough time to lay it down. Distracted by the familiar scent of a McDonald's breakfast somewhere, I lost track of the rest of his rumblings. They took us for a mini tour, complete with a glass divide separating the singer (me) from the producers (them). The interior of the latter space looked like something right out of NASA, and I was assured that no matter what I sounded like, there was enough technology in the space to make it "rock."

Yeah right, I thought . . . we'd see.

I was reminded suddenly of the "We Are the World" video and thought also of *The Simpsons,* guessing that this recording studio was probably somewhere in between.

Collectively, we first listened to the song, sans lyrics, as adapted by Drew's friend's band. I must admit, I was impressed. Very, actually. Gone was anything eighties, and in were the garage-ee sounds of a battle-of-the-bands-winning group. Angry guitar riffs, an even swifter pace than the original, and more than enough edge. Me like-ee.

"Whadayasay we have a listen . . . to your voice," Rog suggested next.

And I was struck with silence.

"Sure," Sheryl peeped. "Where should she—"

"In there." Rog pointed.

I stood up, looked at Sheryl as if she were about to throw me to the wolves, and stepped slowly into that booth area. I couldn't hear them yet, but I saw Rog miming that I place the headset on, which I did and immediately could hear him.

"Just talk right into that mike," he echoed.

"Here?" I said, earnestly trying to follow his instructions.

"Yup."

But I said nothing.

He waved his hand, suggesting that I speak. All I could come up with was, "Hi."

That's when I saw the second guy roll his eyes at the third guy, who shook his head at Sheryl, who proceeded to shrug her shoulders agreeably.

Talk about feeling like an outcast. Yuck.

I got it together and aimed to be pleasing. "What do you suggest, Rog?" I asked, feeling simply ridiculous.

He then, mercifully, began to ask me questions, random ones, to which I'd answer, giving him the vocal ammunition I gathered he would need to set up whatever he had to. His bedside manner was impeccable. Minutes later he told me to come back over and I did, quite happily.

"Now, that wasn't so bad," he said softly.

"Not at all," I breathed.

I was given the lyrics just in case, and after a make-believe stall tactic of a visit to the ladies' room, I was back in there and they, at least, were ready to get started.

As the music came up I felt the first sign of trouble. The song was much faster than the original, which made it necessary for me to put my own spin on the words. Up until then, I had Pat's timing down. I could lip-synch the song perfectly, matching her every word, but this was an unexpected setback. I requested that they play the song for me again, while still in the booth, so I could get a better feel for it. But it was difficult to focus, feeling like I was under the glare of their *I-can't-believe-I'm-doing-this-gig* expressions.

I gave them the thumbs-up, which was a huge huge huge dork move, looked at Sheryl, and we were on our way . . .

And after the first little intro of music, just before Pat would start, I plumb forgot it all. Every last word. "Wait," I said, "wait a minute," and leaned down for the song sheet on the floor. Only to get jackknifed, 'cause the cord to the headset that was on my head was far from long enough.

A comedy of errors, I thought.

I wiped the sweat from my forehead, and again signaled Rog to start. But alas, I missed my opening and we did it again.

And again.

And again.

And again.

"This isn't working," I revealed to a less-than-shocked audience. "Can I come over?" I whimpered.

"Yeah, sure, of course," Rog said, clearly grappling to find his patience.

If I was Rocky, Sheryl was my Mick. She hopped up from her chair, greeted me with a towel, and attempted to console.

"What's the problem?" Rog said.

"I don't know."

There was silence. Deafening silence.

"I think it's 'cause you're all over here and I can see you. It's freaking me out. Can't I do this somewhere else?" I suggested while making eye contact with a door just at the back of the room behind him. "What's that?" I asked.

"What's what?" Sheryl said.

"That." I walked over and opened it up. It was a supply closet and not all that crowded. "How about I sing it in here."

"Where?" Rog turned. "In the storage room???"

His two friends laughed. Sheryl stood silent, not knowing what to do.

"Sure," I said. "Why not?"

"Do you want me to answer that acoustically or would you prefer I just start with the logistics?" he quipped.

I was certain that if I had my privacy I'd be good to go and insisted emphatically that he figure it out.

"Whatever," he barked and he and his team began to make it

happen. Sheryl shook her head, unable to hide her smirk, and I spun around in my chair like a little girl, happy to get my way and now hoping to God I'd be able to deliver.

"Hello? . . . Hello?" I heard from the hallway in the distance. And again, "Hello? Viv? Vivi?"

Oh my God! I thought. *I know that voice.* It was Sophie!!!

And there she was, fresh off a plane, bag in tow, dying to see me, smiling and not knowing what emotions were appropriate in such a foreign and strange place.

"Oh my God Sophie!" I screamed and ran to her. "What are you doing here???"

"Please! Like I was going to miss this? Are you crazy?"

I hugged her like a crazy person. "I love you so much and can't even deal right now. I can't believe you're here!!!" I yelled.

"I know! look!" she squealed, showing me her sparkly very very large ring!

"It's beautiful! Just beautiful! Sophie . . . I can't even . . ."

"I know!" She laughed and we hugged and jumped around like, well, like girls!

Interlocked, I only stopped 'cause she stopped and then I looked where she looked and there were the three of them looking at us, sourly.

"Ummmm. Hey guys, this is Sophie, my best friend. She just surprised me . . . we haven't seen each other in . . . she came from New . . ."

They didn't care.

"Hi. I'm sorry to have interrupted," Sophie said.

"Believe me, you didn't interrupt a thing," Rog said and went back into his closet.

"Okaaaaaay," Sophie whispered, and she and Sheryl greeted and seated.

Before too long they were ready for me. The mike, the headset all wired back to the studio.

"That should do it," Rog said, back to being my best friend. I gathered that he gathered he'd get a lot further and a lot more out of me by being nice.

Soon I was alone. I switched off the lights and shut the door and waited for my cue. Rog was back, though, telling me, patiently, that the door needed to be left open, just a little, so that the wiring wouldn't get screwed up.

And away we went . . .

"Okay Vivian," he said through my headset. "Let's just go though it, all the way, even if you forget a line or a word or something. I just want to record it. Then we'll play it back and take it from there."

"Got it," I said and within seconds the music began . . .

And I made it, the whole way through, I aced it.

Or so I thought, for when I opened the door and stepped out, everyone from Rog-plus-two to Sheryl and Sophie looked as though they had seen a ghost, or, for that matter, heard a monster.

That's when I experienced what true humiliation feels like. I was so turned off by the whole thing I wanted to turn myself inside out. Until I sat there and he played it back. That's when I started to cry, panic-stricken. And that's when Rog-plus-two went out for a cigarette. Why they left was obvious. Before "that" they had thought nothing of smoking the three of us out, over and over and over again.

Sophie just started to laugh and Sheryl followed and then I did, too. Immediately I stopped caring about what the professionals were thinking and instead realized how hilarious this all truly was. Sophie grabbed her handbag and revealed a special duty-free purchase she'd made in the airport in case of emergency.

And there we were, the three of us, taking turns swapping swigs from a bottle of Jack Daniel's!

Desperate times, desperate measures . . .

The rest of the recording session was radically different. Still in the storage room and in the pitch black, sometimes even singing into what I thought was the mike but ended up being a broomstick, I sang Pat's song to the best of my ability. Singing, sometimes, yelling, even screaming, thinking of every guy who ever did me wrong.

It was cathartic. And looking back, had I chickened out, I would have missed one of the best, most classic afternoons of my entire existence.

We used the full five hours, and Rog was still unsure whether he had what he would need to "rebuild me"—think the musical version of *The Bionic Woman*. At least by now we were all friends, and upon leaving I let them know that I felt as though I had slept with each of them. Truly, there was more intimacy in that studio than in all my bedrooms combined.

When Rog invited us to a party later that evening it was me who had to beat Sheryl's answer of yes with a big fat no!

"And why's that?" Rog asked, surprised.

"Oh my God, no offense—but I hope I never see any of you again!" 'Cause there was not a shot in hell that I'd ever be able to face them after what they had seen and heard that afternoon.

"C'mon Viv . . . you were great," he tried.

And I looked at him questioningly. To which he replied lightly, "Okay . . . you're right. Have a nice life."

"You too!" I said and hugged him good-bye.

The car ride back to Shutters was one big cackle. Filled with imitations and recounts of what had transpired. The whole thing was uproarious—and that was only part one!

twenty-six

Trouble in paradise.

There was this absolutely beautiful bridal boutique—"ultra-ethereal" is how she put it—on Robertson that Sophie had heard about or read about somewhere, I think it's called Les Habitudes, and she was desperate to check it out. We stopped first at The Ivy for brunch just because it was the overtly silly thing to do, and also because it's the only meal that I can barely afford to ever eat there. I mean, how much could eggs possibly be??? I invited Sheryl along but she was already out the door, ready to yogatize it with Jacquelyn somewhere.

"Have fun!" I said.

"Dinner tonight, Chaya Venice?" Sheryl asked.

"Oh, definitely. Love it there," I said.

"I'm going to invite Jacks and a few other girls. Is that cool?"

"Sure," I said. "What, like nine?"

"Perfect!" she confirmed. "Have fun with Sophie."

"Thanks, you too." I clicked my phone off and smiled. I was in such a good place emotionally. All my girls, in Los Angeles, it felt too good.

"What's up?" Sophie asked.

"We're gonna do a big girls dinner tonight in Venice," I said. "That was Sheryl."

"Oh, goodie—sounds fun," she said.

We pulled up at The Ivy and valeted just for fun. Behind the miniaturized white picket fence that The Ivy is famous for we sat in their little Garden-of-Eden-ish front outdoor space and spent more time star searching than digesting anything of substance.

I couldn't remember the last time Sophie and I had been to-gether like this. As she yapped on and on about Rob and work and the wedding, it was obvious to me that the gap in our friend-ship I had been dealing with all this time was one-sided. And I was relieved to realize she'd never felt the void. Some might have felt otherwise, but to see her and listen to her, ya just couldn't stop feeling happy and proud. I thought back to that dinner, when I had met Rob and, unfortunately, Grace, too, and I remembered then that more than a slight, I could feel that the nature of our re-lationship was just changing, naturally. *It happens,* I thought, *even to the best of friends,* and I hoped that one day soon it would, in fact, feel natural. That I'd get used to sharing her with someone else. Best friends are like a twenty-four seven hot line but not just in an emergency. When best friends get older and grow, it's still twenty-four seven, only in a different way. You judge more the feeling in your heart than the amount of time you spend talking to them and seeing them. And like everything else, ya learn to make do and deal.

"Okay, enough about me," Sophie stated.

"You sure?" I teased.

"Very funny—not," she said.

"Please tell me that there's someone out here?"

"Come again?"

"Nobody?"

Then I knew where she was going. "Nope," I said rather proudly.

"What's that?"

"What?"

"*Nope!*" she mimicked. "You're boasting."

"Well, I am. I guess. Sort of."

"Why? Look at this place. You're in Los Angeles. You're hanging out with and meeting all these weird creative people—just like you. And do you mean to tell me that that gorgeous room and the grand magnificent bed have only been sleeping one?"

I nodded.

"Wow, Viv, I'm disappointed."

"Why? I mean, don't you think that's a good thing?"

"No! Of course not. That mind of yours!!! Look, I'm not saying that a makeup session won't happen with you and Jack, 'cause it might, but when Rob proposed to me, I just knew it. I just knew that it was right. That he was the one. I mean, he has made me such a happy person—it's like since day one when he walked into my life, everything else just came together and I haven't been the same since."

"So what are you telling me?"

"Well, Vivian, I'm just not sure that Jack is the one that you were meant to be with. And other than that Nick guy . . ."

Wait a second . . . I'd never told her about Nick.

She observed the little riddle in my head and continued, "Yes, I know about Nick and don't be mad because May told me only when we were both discussing you."

"Discussing me?"

"Yeah, Viv, I mean, you've been in like hibernation, total hibernation, and it's a little scary."

"Don't be scared," I remarked rather bitterly.

"I only say this because I worry about you. I don't think it's healthy or possible, honestly, for you to hide away, even though I so understand that you had to. But then you woke up one morning and assumed that you'd made a mistake with him, just assumed it, made yourself believe it, without seeing a single guy in between."

"But . . ."

"But nothing. And Nick doesn't count as a rebound guy. One-nights don't tell you much; they're not supposed to. You should have been and now you definitely need to be dating, Viv, and then, after a little while, revisit the Jack thing."

"Wow, that's a lot to swallow," I said.

"Well, then here," she said, handing me her ice water.

"Cute," I said.

"Thanks."

"Can I be honest with you?"

"Of course." She smiled.

"Ever since Mark I've been confused. NOT about him, but by relationships. I never really recovered from some of the emotional stuff, and I think Jack really got the brunt of all that."

"How so?"

"I never felt as though I would understand them, any of them, after all that with Mark. It's not like I woke up one morning and Mark went from being this great guy to this huge freak, ya know?"

"Uh-huh."

"Everything, when I look back, is in slow motion. I lost my power day by day. It's still a mystery to me. One day he was a challenge, ya know, to get him to like me, and then it was a challenge to get me to leave him. He made me not trust my instinct anymore. About all guys, not just Jack, and I guess I just never felt comfortable falling in love with him. With Jack. I knew he'd never hurt me, physically, but it was like I was always afraid to let it happen. I loved him but not in an intimate, trusting kind of way."

Confused, she said, "But Jack is like the most harmless guy ever. I don't think he has a mean bone in his body."

"I know that, Soph. And that's my point. I never felt worthy of him on some levels, on so many levels really. I never felt like he could understand me. He used to always say that I was 'a rhyme wrapped in a riddle' and I was. I mean, I never understood where all my emotions were coming from, stemming from. And I was terrified that one day he would realize that there was someone out there who was better than me, sweeter than me, kinder than me, simpler than me, and that this whole chase thing, of him trying to get me to commit, once he had me, he'd realize all that. And I'd be left there, knowing better. Knowing that I should never have loved him back."

"Oye," she said.

"I know." I chuckled. "That night when he proposed, there was like this little girl inside of me who was screaming *Yes, yes, yes!* and I was too petrified to let her out. I remember him walking out of my apartment that night and that same voice was yelling, *Stop, stop, stop!* and I silenced her."

"Vivian."

"What?" I said, my eyes welling up with tears.

"I never—"

"I know," I said, "it's okay. It took me a long time to admit all of this to myself. There's no way you could have known. I was showboating through that entire relationship." She grabbed my hand. "I had a lot to sort out afterward, Soph, and I think I'm about done now. I get it."

"So what are you going to do? Because I know you've tried to reach out to him."

"I have faith, Sophie. I don't mean to sound like Oprah or anything here, but I just do."

She looked hesitant.

"I do," I said emphatically. "I've never opened up to him before and that's why I know he'll believe me and give me another chance. I just know it."

"I hope so, Vivi. For your sake I really really do."

"Can we PLEASE change the subject now! Look!" I shouted, "there's Julia Roberts!"

Sophie darted her eyes through every conceivable corner. "Where?"

"I'm kidding," I confessed.

"Ass!"

We paid the bill and walked over to Les Habitudes. It was in fact everything Sophie had said and more. I made the mistake of looking at a price tag on one of the gowns, lost my breath, and started hiccupping.

"Aren't these just heaven?" she squealed.

"Yes. Heav-up-en."

"What do you think?" She pulled me over to an especially satin one, think Shakespeare.

"It's mind-up-blowing Soph. Very Ju-lee-up-et," I said.

My cell phone began to ring and I one-minuted her and walked off to the corner to answer it.

"Hello?" I said not recognizing the number.

"Vivian, it's Reeve." My agent. "There's a glitch, honey." He was referring to the script, I was sure. The network had been sitting with it all week and I had been told that we'd be hearing something any moment now.

"They think it's too female-driven," he admitted disappointedly.

"Too female-driven?" I was confused.

"It's too girl-focused."

"I'm sorry, Reeve, but I mean, I'm a girl. The show's called *Vivianlives*, what am I supposed to do?"

"Listen, kid, I could not agree with you more," he said emphatically. "We all feel that way, but they're paying for the script and they're the ones who have to love it enough to put it on the air."

"So what am I supposed to do now? Is it over?" I feared the worst.

"Nooooooo," he assured me. "It's not over. They're going to fax you some notes this afternoon and you can review them and decide what you want to do."

"What are my options? Sorry, Reeve, but this is all new." (I noticed my hiccups had disappeared—I guess it's true what they say . . . surprise, shock, fear licks them right in the butt!)

"Of course," he said kindly. "First read them over. They could be purely cosmetic and maybe you'll be fine with making some changes. But I warn you—"

"Reeve, hang on a second, I'm sorry." Sophie had the Juliet dress on. She was standing with the seamstress waiting for me.

I put my hand over the phone and walked over to her. "I'm so sorry," I whispered. "You look insane but this is—"

"Don't worry!" she insisted. "I'm not taking this off!!!"

"Okay," I whispered and walked a bit away from them. "Sorry, Reeve, go ahead."

Reeve went on to explain that what was happening with my script was typical. "No one really ever knows what they want," he said, "because what they 'want' is always changing." Already signed with this network, with a script submitted that I truly loved, the next phase could be treacherous. "You can say no and walk away and maintain your artistic beliefs, which I will respect and which I'll totally understand, or you can mold the framework and do what it takes to move ahead. Either way, I think you're fabulous."

I was glad Reeve thought I was fabulous but I wanted him to tell me what to do. And above all else, I wanted to get my hands on those notes. I hung up with him, telling him that I would have something for him tomorrow—an answer, a revised script, only time would tell.

I approached Sophie slowly. This was the first time I'd ever seen her in a wedding dress and I knew this moment was major. She looked like a fairy princess, and the sparkling diamonds in the tiara that the saleswoman had placed in her hair didn't hold a candle to the sparkles emanating from her smile.

"This is it, Vivi! This is so it!" she said first calmly then crazily.

I was speechless.

"What?" she asked nervously. "You don't like it?"

She stared me down, as did the now three saleswomen, and I placed my hands in front, waving their glares off defensively.

"No. Oh my God Sophie . . . it's the most beautiful gown I have ever laid my eyes on."

A collective sigh of relief filled the store.

She rushed me to hand her her purse, which I did, and then she whipped out her credit card and yelped, "I'll take it!"

We both started laughing and giggling and freaking out individually.

"I want to walk out with it. I don't ever want to take it off!" She cried, twirling around.

Sophie bought the tiara, the shoes, the whole kit and caboodle.

Sheryl and Jacquelyn met us at Les Habitudes and Jacquelyn, which was hilarious, fell to the floor when she first laid eyes on it.

After all the kvetching goggling was over, Sophie handed me a gown—it was, of course, a dusty rose color—that looked more like a wedding dress dyed pink than anything else. "Soph?" I said, "what's this?" to which she replied, "It's the perfect dress for my maid of honor." And then I lost it.

And after I'd tried it on, unbeknownst to me, Sophie had bought it. I won't even tell you what it cost. Her reality is very different from mine. But a fine reality just the same!

Soon after, we crossed the street and shared fruit-infused shakes at News Room. While Sophie called her mother and then Rob and while Jacquelyn touched base with her sitter, I caught Sheryl up on my conversation with Reeve.

"What are you still doing here?" she whispered, frustrated.

"What am I supposed to do?" I whispered right back.

"Sophie?" Sheryl asked. "Wanna go for facials at Fred Segal Beauty?" She winked over at me.

"Oh my God—yes!" she responded predictably. "Viv, is that cool?"

"Of course," I said. "But I'm going to go back to Shutters; I have some work to do. You're in good hands with these women," I assured her.

"We'll be back by six, six thirty," Sheryl said.

With that, I said my good-byes and walked back to The Ivy to fetch my car. There, while waiting, I could have sworn I saw Julia Roberts.

twenty-seven

Back at the ranch, my ranch, I placed the Polaroid of Sophie and me that the saleswoman had taken on my bedside table and noted the lengthy fax that screamed *oh boy* on my desk. Before dealing with the verdict on my script I picked up the photo once more and basked in it. There we were with more taffeta between us then a gaggle of girls on prom night. Sophie, jolly and in all her glory, and me a bit awkward with a forced smile, given the surreal quality of the moment. I wondered, too, for a second, if I could simply dye my maid-of-honor dress white should I ever find myself strutting down an aisle of my own. That's how unbelievably gorgeous it was. Think Halle Berry on Oscar night. Simply spectacular.

I changed out of my jeans and hoodie and into, yes, you guessed it, "the bathrobe." I put my hair up in a pony, grabbed a Hawaiian Punch from the mini bar and a swirly straw from my purse. (I'd bought some at the gas station a few hours before. I hadn't seen one in years and, well, I love 'em!) I grabbed the fax and a pen from my desk and sat outside again on my terrace. Evening was lurking and that was my favorite time of day, watching the sunset. Instant relaxation. I put my feet up, took a sip of my punch, and got on with it.

Immediately I was put off by what looked like bitter teacher's notes in overdrive. Cross-outs everywhere, small thought bubbles from side to side. Page after page. At the end there were more specific notes explaining how "the brother" needs to play a larger part. The "boyfriend" needs a bigger role, and what about the "manager" of the coffee shop, can't she be a he?

They had turned my show into a younger version of *Friends;* they wanted six main characters, three guys, three girls. I took a moment to swallow that.

MOMENT.

I was disappointed at first and then angry. The whole idea was to not be something that was already out there. And why try? *Friends* was so good at being *Friends.* Now, mind you, there was not a black or white obvious statement telling me this, but you'd have to be living in Oz to think otherwise. Furthermore, as their notes suggested, they wanted more shopping, more sexual innuendos, and then my mind went to *Sex and the City* and again, I realized that they had missed the whole point.

I mean, why commission the script in the first place, ya know? We could have gone to another network that would have loved everything we stood for??? None of this was making sense. And it wasn't like I was furious and ready to walk, not at all; I would have been crazy to even consider that as an option. I thought that finding a happy medium would be the most sensible thing to do. If I acknowledged every single note and suggestion, they'd be buying a totally different show, and I doubted highly that that would please them, either. I could so see Reeve calling me back after such changes only to say that they thought it was too close to *Friends* and too much like *Sex and the City.*

I called two of the producers from Crowning Productions, knowing that they had received the same documents and hoping that they would offer up some wise advice and useful suggestions.

But after a forty-five-minute conversation we were all at a loss, and again they threw the decision to me. "It's your story," they said. Which I really admired. They had all this money on the line and had spent all this time with me. I thought it was way cool of them not to push me into a direction I wasn't comfortable with. It really made me see how much they believed in my story and my better judgment. (That doesn't happen very often in the entertainment world, I gather.)

So I went with it, going back inside and onto my computer, sending an e-mail to everyone involved as to the direction I planned to go postnotes. I clicked SEND feeling scared, knowing in the back of my mind that the changes they were suggesting were not minor aesthetic ones, or structural; what they wanted was an entirely different show with our original title. *Too many cooks in the kitchen,* I thought.

I sat at the foot of my bed feeling defeated. And I tried to talk myself out of it, weighing the pros and cons. Would it be that horrible if the show ended up being something different than I had imagined? No. It would be triumphant regardless, an uber-cadoober (just made up that word, meaning "extremely uber!") achievement and so so fun. However, and this is a big *however,* I didn't think it would stand a chance. I'd give them what they wanted and they'd pass, 'cause it wouldn't be special anymore. I didn't need a crystal ball to tell me that.

But ya know what, I'd been wrong so many times before about tons of different things. I mean, this is what they did for a living day in and day out. They had to know what they were talking about, right? So I found a slight smile and remained cautiously optimistic as Sophie came through the door, nearly camouflaged by shopping bags.

"I love L.A.," she stated, dropping her things on the floor and jumping onto the bed. "Is this like the best place or what?"

I smiled.

"What's the matter?"

"It's work. It's nothing. Whadya get?" I mean, tell me, what's more fun than shopping if not laying out your recent purchases and discussing them to the bone?

The girl had done some damage but I'd expected nothing less.

Her cell phone rang as I was salivating over a chino linen motorcycle jacket.

"Awww, baby, I miss you, too," she purred. "Oh my God, V," she whispered, "he said that every second feels like an hour!"

Oh my God, I mouthed. (And subconsciously upchucked.) *Smile.* I thought. *Smile.*

While she talked I got dressed. Our dinner reservation was fast approaching. I found a clean pair of jeans and my last white tank top and stared less than passionately at my less-than-lifeless clothing options lying inside my closet. That's when that jacket I had been admiring was thrown at me. Sophie was still talking on my bed but urging me to try it on via hand signals.

Perfect fit.

"You sure?" I asked.

She nodded yes. And I was immediately injected with a good mood. I went for my black boots when Sophie clicked her phone off and pulled out my olive strappies. "It's so about these," she said.

"Ya think?" I asked only to receive a glare that said, *You're kidding me, right?*

It was another amazing evening complete with perfect hair weather and a mischievous breeze in the air. We drove through the last bit of Santa Monica en route to pick up Sheryl and crew at Jacquelyn's place. While stopped at a dainty traffic light Sophie confided, "Viv, I've got to tell you something . . ."

My hands clenched the steering wheel.

"As much as I like Sheryl . . . I'm a little jealous."

This was shocking, but also very humbling.

"Aww, Soph."

"I am. I feel like, well, you know that just because I don't see you all the time—"

"Sophie, stop. I know."

This was a moment a little too drenched in sweetness and cuteness for me, although it was still gratifying in a slightly selfish way.

Soon enough, my little Saab was jam-packed with girlies and it felt like I was zapped back into time—think high school, the lone girl with her license. Such fun!

"I love having you guys here!" Jacquelyn proclaimed. "I feel like I have my singlehood back!!"

"We're happy to oblige!" Sheryl commented and then we all oohed and ahhed it over Sophie's wedding gown.

She had just finished describing her dress when Sheryl announced, "Vivian, guess what I'm holding in my hand?"

I turned around, tried to make it out, and nearly drove into a tree. "Please, Sheryl, just divulge, I wanna make it to my wedding!" Sophie pleaded.

"Hey, have you guys heard that new song . . . the remake of that classic . . ."

I pulled the car over in the middle of moving traffic.

"Give it to me!" I shouted over the screams of my friends in the background.

"Nope," she said.

"Sher, seriously."

"Or what, V? We want to hear it!"

"Aw, Viv, let's have a listen!" Sophie suggested convincingly.

"I can't."

"Aww, c'mon Vivian," Jacquelyn said.

I opened my car door and began to step out onto the sidewalk. "You guys can, 'cause honestly, I can't deal with the whining."

I expected them, at least one of them, to take pity on me, but to my surprise not one of them did. I walked off as the intro music started to play and then I heard my voice and I wanted to die. And then I heard them all screaming and cracking up and I turned around, curiously, and surprisingly, 'cause I wanted to hear it, too. And even more so, wanted to get in on all their fun.

They were just freaking out, trying to listen but barely able to. Oh, the screaming, the smiling, the dying. It was contagious. They turned the volume up as high as it would go and Sophie jumped out of the car and started dancing and singing and I was somewhere in between. Trying to listen, trying to dance, but every time I heard my oh-so-terrible voice stretching to the max, hearing the effort, the invisible chorus mysteriously digitized, I was amazed and humiliated. We all just looked at each other in shock. And finally, when we all just couldn't take it anymore, we hopped back into my abandoned car and took deep breaths and wiped the tears from the corners of our eyes. Sheryl was afraid she was having a heart attack.

We arrived for dinner nearly thirty minutes late. We must have listened to "Heartbreaker" more than a dozen times. While it was happening I remember so clearly knowing that I would never forget the moment—ever. It would be a moment that I would forever compare others to. It was pure. And that's why I knew that doing it was the right move. I had nothing to lose and absolutely everything to gain. And those thirty minutes encapsulated every decision I had ever made.

It's one of my fondest memories.

twenty-eight

The next day I drove Sheryl and Sophie back to LAX and got homesick all over again. I tried not to let my emotions show as I waved them good-bye and quickly sped out of there before either turned around. They both knew me better than to get offended.

As I left it with Sheryl, I requested that she spare me any feedback from the "Heartbreaker" single. It either would or would not make the album, and I would find out just like anyone else would. After some clever negotiating I got her to agree.

I spent the next three days huddled in my room reworking the script. The network executives and the producers at the studio had given me the green light via e-mail and with that, I slowly put the puzzle that was my original concept and the recent notes together.

In moments of frustration and/or exhaustion, I would grab a towel and walk out to the beach. Californians take their sand for granted, I thought; I was the lone oceangoer for long stretches to my right and left at each time. Every once and again an eager surfer or a young mother with her infant would enter and exit the landscape, but for all intents and purposes I was totally on my own.

I tried Jack on one of these occasions and again, his number was disconnected. Without a forwarding one to reference, I would play out our conversation in my mind. Several times I thought of keeping an individualized diary of these pseudo-discussions, but between the second novel and the edited script, my fingertips were throbbing.

I also thought back to Sophie's take, both on my reveal and on my social-slash-personal life. I for one know that I can be pretty convincing when I want to be, and so I thought about it all again, weighing my rationale. While soaking up the sun (and working out my stomach muscles: Someone once told me that contracting your abdominals for long repeated stretches of time is always worthwhile, whenever and wherever), I decided to again try to think and live like a single person. The rest of my stay in L.A. would no longer be a twisted version of a peace offering to Jack. I thought that it couldn't hurt to be more open-minded and that perhaps I would stand to benefit or grow or learn something in the interim.

I was also taken aback when I thought about how Jack had usurped my thoughts over the last year. Unknowingly and innocently on his part, I was aware of that, but I had just never experienced being so obsessed over a guy before. Back and forth, back and forth, constantly. And that made me wonder how much of what I knew to be true and accurate and justified really was. I think that when any of us obsesses about someone, we can't help but romanticize, twisting the reality of the relationship and our feelings into something more than what they are. Hoping to not suffer from a lonely-girl delusion, I again vowed to seek him out after I returned to New York and once I was absolutely and positively one hundred percent without a shadow of a doubt sure.

On the fourth day I drove back to Crowning and reviewed my script at a scheduled roundtable meeting. The reactions were positive, but I could tell that I was definitely not the only person with reservations.

"We're going to have this punched up before we give it to the network," Reeve mentioned toward the end of the meeting. By this point I knew what he meant. A seasoned, schooled writer would be commissioned to incorporate one-liners throughout. Joke telling was not my forte. And that was fine with me. After a deafening moment of silence, I chose to voice a concern for the record.

"I worked hard to do what was asked of me here," I explained to nods and looks of appreciation and agreement. "But that said, I also am concerned: Are we really doing the right thing?"

That's when Elaine, the most respected producer in the room, offered the following: "It's a gamble, Vivian. And we've all been down this road before. And I really feel that what you've come up with is that happy medium you referred to in your initial e-mail. I, personally, would rather give them this and best-case scenario, if given the chance, steer the show back to our original vision, once we're on the air."

Again, a collective confirmation by the majority at the table.

"The important thing here is that you did not sell out. Your voice is still here and that's what we all believed in from day one." She winked my way and said her good-byes. She and practically everyone else was off to another meeting somewhere in la-la land.

Reeve walked me to my car. "So when are you outta here, kiddo?" he asked.

"If it's all right with you, I'd like to get a flight sometime tomorrow. Unless, of course, you need me to stick around. I can absolutely do that; just give me the word," I said.

Together we leaned on my car, kind of wrapping things up.

"So if they get the script on Monday, Tuesday, we'll either get word right away or they'll take their time with it. It's usually either an immediate decision or a merciless wait," he explained.

"Jeez," I said, breathing deeply. "It's so much pressure. How you do this over and over is beyond me."

"I know it. But for a numbers guy like me who always wanted to be in the business but without a creative bone in my entire body, I love being around it. I love taking someone through it, it's a rush every time."

"So what do you think our chances are?" I asked. "Be honest."

"I'm not going to lie to you, Vivian. It's fifty–fifty. But what you need to understand is that those are great odds in this business. You've got to believe!"

I gave him a look that said I'd try, hard as it might be. Reeve said that if things went well, I would need to be back here within the month. That Crowning would set me up with an apartment, a car, the whole nine if we went to pilot. A smile took over my face; what he was describing sounded incredible. And the fact that I would be paid, and very well I might add, was what scared me the most. Not wanting to get too psyched 'cause if it didn't go, I'd be wrecked. Shooting the pilot would mean another twelve weeks at least, he said. What terrible news, right—hardly!!!

"And what if it doesn't go?" I asked.

"You mustn't ever think that way," he said. "Ever."

I thanked him profusely, for everything. He'd made the whole experience a lot less bumpy than it could have been. He told me to call Terry, his assistant, when I got back to my hotel; she'd get my itinerary and flight all squared away. We exchanged our good-byes and when I pulled up alongside his car—I was going left, he was going right—he signaled for me to roll down my window. With his shades on and his convertible top down, he shouted, "Love the ride, Vivian! It's all an adventure!"

I smiled back seasick-ish-ly and he drove away.

That's just about when things got crazy.

twenty-nine

I had checked out of Shutters, bags packed, towels and soaps swiped, gas tank filled, and stopped at a Jamba Juice for one last hoorah. When my cell phone rang unexpectedly, it was Terry, Reeve's assistant.

"Vivian?" she questioned nervously.

"Yeah?"

"Are you on your way?"

"Yeah?"

"She already left!" she shouted, presumably to Reeve.

"Tell her to pull over!" I heard him holler back.

"Reeve wants you to pull over," she said. But something about her tone had made me do so before his instruction.

"Done," I said.

"Hang on, I'll put you through," she said. "Hang on just a minute."

I sat there on the 405 as speeding cars passed one after the other, shaking my little car to and fro. At first I was sure it was bad news—that somehow someway the network had received the script and decided NO, already. That Reeve did not want me at the wheel for news like that. Still waiting, I tossed around the idea of the YES. That again, somehow someway the network had received the script and decided YES, already.

"Vivian," Reeve said decidedly. "You need to come back to Los Angeles."

"What? Why?"

"Nothing to do with the show," he said flat-out, not to prolong my obvious first would-be thought. "I was on the phone late yesterday with Elaine as a fax came across my desk—"

"Okay???"

"And the fax was from Lou Lou Cameron." He said her name as though it were *Madonna* and that I would be able to put the pieces together from there. After a beat he realized that I hadn't a clue and spelled the rest out for me.

I'll bottom-line you:

Lou Lou Cameron was the premier casting director in the entire town. She had been responsible for placing no-name actors and actresses in their first breakout roles. Actors and actresses who would later become huge box-office sensations, demanding tens of millions of dollars per picture. She had exclusive deals with filmmakers like Cameron Crowe and Steven Spielberg, to name just two.

"Great," I said. "How nice for her. But how does that have anything to do with me, Reeve?"

"Well, it doesn't, yet . . . See, the fax was a shout out to a select number of agents, looking for a brunette in her mid- to late twenties, and a no-name, to play the supporting co-lead in Dave Leone's next movie."

Note: I knew exactly who Dave Leone was. He was a writer-slash-director whose movies I knew line by line. I had them on DVD. He was *the* impresario of romantic comedy.

My heart started to race 'cause I had a vague idea as to where Reeve was headed . . .

"And so I threw it out to Elaine. I read her the character sum-

mary, asked her if she had heard about the film, did she k̶
had been cast in the lead, et cetera."

"Yeah?"

"And I said aloud, wow, this girl sounds like our Vivian, to which
Elaine said that she was thinking the very same thing."

"But—" I tried.

"But nothing. Hang on . . . So on a whim, I had Terry send over
your bio and your press and that tape we have of you—"

"You did not!"

"And, which hardly comes as a surprise to me, she now wants to
meet you first thing Monday morning."

I breathed deeply before I said a word . . .

"Now, Reeve, you know I'm not an actress."

"Doesn't matter," he responded abruptly.

"It doesn't?"

"Nope."

"What the hell," I said. "It's just a meeting right? Like a hello. This
is me. This is what I look like. This is what I sound like—"

"Partially."

"How do you mean?"

"Well, you'll have to read for her."

"Read what?" I asked hypercautiously.

"Your lines."

Oh God.

"Like act?" I said as stupidly as you might imagine.

He laughed. "It's less than a page of dialogue, and you'll have
a stand-in who will read opposite you. I looked the lines over, it's
nothing too terrible. Terry faxed them over along with the directions
to your appointments and to the audition."

"Faxed to where, my glove compartment?" I looked around at
the gray crowded highway and the rain that was pouring down.

"No. Back to Shutters. You're booked there through Tuesday.
Turn that car around, kiddo."

ht.

ck to Santa Monica, Reeve went on: "Debbie's

s Debbie?"

vian. From now till Monday afternoon. You're

"I am?" Half laughing.

"Yup. You're from Kentucky and you're a checkout girl at the supermarket."

I had one hand over my mouth in disbelief.

"You're agonizing over your boyfriend, a struggling writer who has two small kids."

"Wait. I have kids?"

"No, Duane, your boyfriend, does. They live with you and when you're not working, you take care of them. He's barely ever around and you've begun to think that he might be using you as a full-time babysitter with benefits." He laughed.

"Hang on!" I laughed, too, nervously. "You mean to tell me that you read this, and read it to Elaine, and you both thought I'd be perfect for this role???" I said, horrified, and then I rambled, "It would be one thing if you were looking for a neurotic New Yorker who worked in . . . I don't know, advertising or something. But, Reeve, I mean—"

"Oh, and it says here that you have to audition with the accent." He couldn't help but laugh at the sound of it.

"Oh great. Genius. Perfect. I think I'm going to wet my pants."

"Not to worry. Terry has you booked with . . . let me see . . . a dialogue coach on Saturday and an acting coach on Sunday."

"Of course she does."

"I have to take this," he said, referring to another call. "I'll ring you over the weekend. It's a goof, Vivian. The chances are slim, but it's worth you staying and meeting Lou Lou, don't you think?"

"I—I—"

"And besides," he concluded, "it's great for the books."

If I had a dollar . . .

Listen, I couldn't make this shit up if I tried. The best I figure is that if you put yourself out there and move with the energy of the earth, things happen. All the while, being yourself, maintaining your honesty, and listening to your spirit twenty-four seven. Sure, this particular thing was way out there and insanely far-fetched but it came to me. Landed in my lap unexpectedly and what was I supposed to do? Pretend I didn't want to give it a try? After the singing, I didn't have much self-respect to lose anyway.

There were a few times when I thought about not going through with it. But when I thought about the evening where I'd undoubtedly be sitting in the theater, a few years from now, at Dave Leone's latest film, and seeing Debbie on the big bad screen, I'd be sick with regret not knowing what might have happened. And to me, that image was far worse than not getting the role and making a huge fool of myself during the audition process. Right???

Hmmmmmm.

That weekend was wretched.

I had butterflies in my stomach throughout and struggled desperately to not crack up as I was introduced to the world of acting by one patient coach after the next. Endlessly self-conscious. It really wasn't for me.

I had to fax the lines, what the industry calls "sides," along with my appointments to my friends and family to get them to believe me. And at night, when I would try to shut my eyes and find a little sleep, it was nearly impossible.

If you don't previously have a dream or an ambition, the thought of it not coming to fruition is harmless. But now this was yet another opportunity, a fantastic insane once-in-a-lifetime opportunity, that I would attempt and, of course, now want. Was I ready to fail at something else? At something new? Something I'd never dreamed of wanting? Something I'd never have thought I'd be a candidate for? That's what kept me up on Sunday night. Knowing that the chances were pretty high that it wouldn't pan out and that either way I would wind up seated in a darkened movie theater seeing the film anyway, having tried and failed, and feeling shitty just the same.

What? That's valid.

On deck was my show, the record, my first book, and soon my second . . . *thick-skinned* ain't the word. And I hadn't even gotten back to New York yet.

thirty

The last and final perk of my Hollywood hiatus was a first-class seat home. Ahhhh, what a dream. Five-course dinner, top-notch service, and room enough for two, three even. I got myself seated and was pretty sure that I could never be a coach girl again. Fat chance, but I digress.

Seated on my plane were Amanda Peet, just in front of me, and Jack Wagner, just across. It took every bit of will that I had not to sing aloud, "All I need—is just a little more time—to be sure what I feel—is it all in my mind." Oh my God! I'm not kidding. My inner volume was turned way up. Besides, "Jessie's Girl," Jack's little ballad, was at the top of Sophie's and my all-time-favorite cheesy-eighties-songs list. How many times did that little tune rage from my boom box! I kept looking at him, hearing the song, scared he'd used his celebrity strings to get me bumped back to coach! *Get a grip Vivian,* I demanded of myself, *get a grip!*

Seated next to me was a dear older lady named Evelyn, although she insisted that I call her Eve. We got acquainted as everyone else around us slept. (It was a red-eye flight.) She was traveling to New York to see her grandchildren. She was a ballerina, she said, in her teens and twenties, and her husband, Philip, now deceased, had been a violinist. They traveled around the world until they each reached their sixties and you could just tell, factoring in the way she spoke and the way she carried herself, that she had hundreds of stories to tell. What started out as a generalization, when she asked me what I did and if I was married, ended up being an hour's worth of meaningful discussion. She had so much wisdom and encouragement. She seemed so proud of me, proud the way my own grandmother would be.

She conveyed the importance of love in all of it. How it would all mean nothing at the end of the day if I passed up the love of my life in the process. Which, as you would probably guess by now, I promised I would not do. But her eyes, as they lay behind her thick but still chic, Lisa-Loeb-inspired frames, were not convinced. "Trust me dear, I know what I'm talking about," she emphasized, halting a quick sip of her tomato juice to drive her point home.

I helped Eve retrieve her things from baggage claim and escorted her to her family in waiting. Before she could even introduce me, she was engulfed in family, shouting "Nana! Nana!" and I thought it was more appropriate that I get on my way.

By the time I reached Manhattan it was almost nine A.M. I knew that if I were to first go home, I'd crash and burn. For one thing, I hadn't slept, and second, I hadn't seen my Omelet in almost fourteen weeks. Leaving him again after a frenzy-filled hello wouldn't suit either of us all that well. So instead I instructed my driver to drop me and my things off at my office. I figured I'd get some stuff done, catch up on a few things, and then do "home" just right.

The day was a frenzy and by two I had to call it quits. I was sick of hearing my own voice, telling the same story. On some levels, I felt that the more I talked about it, the fewer the chances that any of it would materialize into more than, well, than just that, a chance.

Stan and his underlings made no bones about telling me what the success of the show would mean to the business. As if I hadn't considered that ever before. "Lay it on thick!" I joked, scooping myself out of his uber-modern and efficiently uncomfortable Swedish chair. "I did the best I could do, Stan. That's it. We'll just have to see."

"Well, I hope so," he whined, sporting a forced smile that made him look nauseous.

I had Jayden messenger my luggage and the rest of my notes and "homework" over to my apartment, as I expected to not be back at work for another day or so. I shed the pointed flippy flats that I had picked up in Beverly Hills for my cozy black Chuck Taylors that had a permanent spot beneath my desk. I phoned Joseph telling him that I'd be home in less than thirty and with that I was outta there.

Then it was back on the subway, in dirty denim jeans, a heather-gray long-sleeved T-shirt, and a messenger bag filled with magazines, receipts, my (new) wallet, my (new) cell phone, and my house keys, sans a single trapping of my experiences out West.

I couldn't wait to get home. Despite even that I had redecorated it in my head a thousand times. Despite that my mailbox key never worked on the first try, that my feuding neighbors drove me crazy, that my ceilings were water-stained and my wood floors were mangled by what I believed to be close to fifty cats that had probably inhabited the place before me. Even though my air-conditioning only enjoyed pumping cool air into the apartment during fall's months and the same, in reverse, went for my heater; even though it was four long flights up without an elevator; still, I couldn't wait to get there.

I skipped and jumped up to my place with my last bit of energy. I found my keys, eventually, and was ready for the welcome to end all welcomes. But when I stepped inside, there was no one to greet me.

"Omelet! Joseph!" I shouted. I thought it was strange and quickly assumed I had missed them outside; Joseph had probably taken him out for me. *That's nice*, I thought. But when I saw Omelet's brown leather leash I was very confused.

"Omelet! Joseph!" I repeated.

And then I heard the TV coming from my bedroom and it all began to make sense.

"Hey!" I said opening the door and quickly thereafter, I decided to remove it. I mean the door. I loathe surprises. The last surprise that had beckoned behind my bedroom door was Jack's proposal, remember? And that, regrettably, did not hold a candle to this one:

There on my bed was Joseph with Omelet lying to his left. Omelet was not even aware that I had entered my room. One of his eyes, bloodshot and streaked with pus, was caved into the socket. Thankfully his fur hid what must have been happening to him underneath. I would later learn the term: *atrophy:* a wasting or decrease in size of a body organ, tissue, or part owing to disease, injury, or lack of use: *muscular atrophy of a person affected with paralysis.* And I swear to you that had I not seen him blink his other eye I would have thought he was dead.

I looked at my brother, who finally looked back only to say softly, "Omelet has cancer, sis."

I'll skip over my initial reaction.

thirty-one

Hearing the word *cancer* when it thankfully is not attached to you or a loved one is still, for the moment and for whatever duration of time after, completely devastating. You feel empathy for the victim and the victim's family. And you look forward to the day that some bizarrely intelligent doctor gets on the news to announce that a cure has finally been found.

But to search for a word or a group of words that are meant to mirror your feelings when it pertains to you, your life as you know it, your loved one, is impossible. And believe me I've tried. I just closed my thesaurus realizing that no word could ever suffice.

Instead all I can tell you is that beyond the horror of the news, I felt helpless. It was a death sentence, as Omelet's cancer had been detected in its final stages and all they could do was medicate him. (This was the report I got from Joseph and later, from my parents, who drove in from Pennsylvania that night.)

My family thought it best to not worry me while I was away, a decision that initially infuriated me but, after time, I came to understand. The vet had given Omelet two to six months, so my family felt certain that I would be home before any final decisions would need to be made.

While I can understand that Omelet is my pet, he's a dog, an animal, not a human being, I could in no way explain that to my heart. I couldn't imagine my life without his companionship and pure unconditional love, and again, I had the idea that I had somehow let him down, was unable to save him.

That afternoon also made me think, for the first time in all our years together, that he, regardless of cancer, would not live forever. That, as it goes, I would for all intents and purposes outlive him. And I was relieved that this marked the first occasion. For the thought of it physically made my heart sink to the floor and my throat snap shut. And for several moments, too, I hated him. I hated that he had come into my life and been so good to me and for me. I hated my emotional attachment to him and wished that that damn dilapidated station wagon had never pulled up to that diner that day. I thought that I should have opted for a fish, a few fish maybe, pets that I could never snuggle with, that wouldn't take on my emotions and comfort me. Pets that wouldn't kiss me good-bye and smother me hello. And I was angry because I knew no one would ever understand what he meant to me and how much losing him would be a void irreplaceable.

But when I walked toward him and saw him wag his tail ever so slightly I couldn't sustain my fury for too long. Instead I hugged him and petted him, told him that we'd find a cute but not too girly eye patch for him, and that I would feed him beef shank and junk-food-based treats whenever he wanted and I would give him "my side" of the bed from here on out. And that I wouldn't ever leave him again.

And when I knelt down toward his furry fuzzy face and rubbed my warm nose against his cold one and he surprised me with a bunch of quick licks and wiped my tears, inadvertently or not (I think not), from my face, well, again, there really are no right words.

My parents stayed with me for the next several days, and

through it all we got on incredibly well. Until my father caught an un-expected glimpse of my tattoo and nearly lost it. But my mother calmed him down and I'm quite sure he'll pick up where he left off one of these days.

I decided not to involve my friends and coworkers with Omelet's condition, only because after I spoke to Sophie, her sweet words of understanding made me feel it all over again. There was too much at stake for me to be an emotional wreck and I knew that this can-cer could easily be my tipping point. I just couldn't have that.

I went back to my vet with Omelet to get the lowdown and make sure that there was no suitable and realistic treatment out there for him. And gingerly, the doctor explained his condition. Yes, I could put Omelet through a series of painful procedures; but with less than a five percent chance of success, he said, that would make Omelet's last months with me the worst of his little life. The doc-tor urged me not to think selfishly in this matter. That while I might want him to be with me as long as possible, *as long as possible* could be inhumane. There would come a time, he said, when I would "just know" that Omelet was ready.

The doctor upped his dose of cortisone, warned me of the side effects, and said, delicately, that every case is different, unleashing a tiny thread of hope that Omelet's time here could be longer than even he could predict.

I grabbed hold of that statement and took Omelet to the dog run. He was greeted by all his friends as I went basically ignored, which was customary. Either way, I loved being home. Being with him. Being in the city. Sitting at the run. It felt natural. I hadn't given much thought to any of what was looming on my horizon because then, it all felt make-believe. Being home, around my family, in my apartment, close to my friends, that was who I was, that's who I am, and at the end of the day was what was truly important. All the other "stuff" was just gravy. It was then that I realized how unbal-anced my life had been up until that point. I had neglected so much. So many people and so many parts of myself. Everything was about me, my angst, and especially my work. I hid behind it. Maybe they called it la-la land for a reason—a reason that I was slowly beginning to understand. Key word: *slowly*. I was coming down from the point of view that somehow, it had to be all or nothing. That to be a huge success, to myself and to others, I would have to sacrifice so much. But now, I knew I couldn't. I knew that the scent I was picking up had a name. It was called *balance*. For someone as layered as me, the onion, as the movie *Shrek* so sweetly and simply points out, when Donkey (voiced by Eddie Murphy) tells Shrek (Mike Myers) that he's an onion, when he's torn up over his emotions and he doesn't know why, well anyway, I would never survive, no matter what, without the crux of the world that I had known for all my time—the onion.

On our walk home, I tried to figure out the best way for me to immortalize Omelet. It wasn't a depressing notion; it was a surprisingly happy one. A photo? A painting? A poem? Nothing seemed right. I wanted to always have him close to me, to my heart, and so none of the above seemed appropriate. And that's when it dawned on me. I would get a mold of Omelet's paw, ask one of the art directors to scan it, and then take it to a jeweler. Maybe make a gold casting of it, the size of a quarter maybe, and wear it on a chain around my neck. Yup! That was so it.

As crazy as this may sound, after I got his eye patch, sourced out the way in which to make my necklace, and saw the difference in Omelet after we increased his meds—I'm talking a matter of days here—I was delirious with denial!

Hey, whatever works.

thirty-two

With still no word from Cali-fornia, I kept to business as usual. I had just left what felt like the bazil-lionth meeting with Supreme Vodka. Yup. The scary guy with white teeth from the boat. Some many months later, we got the deal. They would be our new client as soon as the ink dried on our contract. And it was a relief, 'cause it was a lucrative six-month relationship with options for extension should we meet their expectations. Both Drew's and Sheryl's faces looked new when we, finally able to react, rejoice, and yap it up, got outside their corporate offices in Mid-town. As Sheryl phoned Stan and company and Drew lit up a ciga-rette, I saw a very familiar face approaching me on Park Avenue, and I could tell that face felt the same about me. In a matter of sec-onds I was greeting Tom, Jack's very best friend.

"Vivian Livingston, well, what do you know!" he exclaimed.

"Tom!"

We hugged and sized one another up noticeably.

"It's been—" he started.

"—a very long time," I finished.

Drew interrupted with a quick hello and told me that he and

Sheryl would be grabbing a celebratory cocktail at Café St. Barts just a few blocks away.

"Take your time!" Sheryl said as they walked away.

"So," I said, "how are you? It's great to see you, Tom."

"Gosh," he replied, almost giddy, "I don't even know where to start."

"Anywhere," I said. "From the beginning!"

"Well, we're pregnant!"

"You and Lisa?"

"Of course."

"Congratulations, I didn't know . . ."

"Thanks. Thanks Vivian. The wedding's not till next summer, after the baby is born, you know how Lisa is, she doesn't want a little pouch sewn into her wedding dress."

"Which is understandable," I offered.

"And, you know, my Irish Catholic parents are still dealing with that but, hey, you can't please everyone, right?"

"That's right." I nodded.

"And how about you? Lisa brought your book home and got through it in one night!"

"Really?" I said, uncomfortably.

"Of course. She bought it the first day it went on sale. I went with her. There was this great big display right when we walked into the bookstore . . . congratulations, Vivian, you must be so proud!"

"Kinda," I squirmished.

There was an awkward silence where we both just grinned. He knew that I wanted to ask him about Jack. I knew that he knew that. And I could tell that he wanted to broach the same topic and he knew that I knew it. It was one of those . . .

And immediately thereafter we both went in for the kill, managing to jinx ourselves in the process.

"I'm sorry. You go," I joked.

"No, no, you."

"How is he?" I asked nervously. "Jack. How is he?"

He took a moment before he answered knowing full well, even for a guy, how important his response was. How every word would matter and be dissected in more ways than one. He even unbuttoned the lone button on his suit jacket before beginning.

"He's . . . good."

Disappointed, I mumbled, "Good. That's good. I'm glad he's good." Then after a beat I just went for it. "I miss him," I confessed, with my eyes to the pavement. "I really really miss him."

"Look, Vivian, you know I think you're great," he said, almost consoling me. "But Jack, well, you know, he's a simple guy. He just wants what we all want, ya know."

"Sure," I said dejectedly.

"You guys are just at different places in your lives."

I began to sense tears and was not about to start bawling in the middle of a packed Park Avenue during happy hour. I fought them off like dogs, staring at the crinkles in Tom's forehead as a focus.

"Vivian?"

"Yeah?"

"Are you all right?"

"Sure? Why?"

"Well, because unless I've got a memo attached to my scalp . . . ," he said awkwardly.

I tried to look at him but I couldn't. Instead I looked behind him and over at the nameless nine-to-five-ers that passed. "It's just . . . a lot, ya know."

"How do you mean?"

"I made a big mistake, Tom." And once those words left my mouth it was impossible to keep the tears back.

He repositioned himself and put his briefcase down.

"Listen, Vivian, everything happens for a reason."

"Yeah, the reason is I was an idiot!" and then that was it. Tom picked up his briefcase and walked me over to the lobby of the building I had just come from and at that point I didn't care. This was as real and as vivid as any of my fantasies as where Jack was concerned. I had to let it out. Talking about it with Sophie, with Omelet, with Evelyn on the freakin' plane was just talking, it was rubbish. Getting it off my chest with Tom was as close to Jack as I had come and my heart simply took over.

"I know he has a girlfriend but I want . . . him back," I confessed. "I've called him, I've written him—"

"I know." He cut me off. "I know."

"Wait? You mean he got my messages, he got my letter? Please tell me. Tell me."

"Yes, he did. And we talked about it. He didn't know what to do. How serious you were. You can understand that, right?"

"Yes," I said sniffling.

"It's just that, well, she's good for him," he said. "It's easy."

"I'm sure," I said half bitterly.

"Look, I'll be honest with you Vivian . . . He got that invite for your party . . ."

"Yeah?"

"And he went."

"Yeah, I thought so. Someone had said that they thought they'd seen him there."

"Both Lisa and I told him it was a good idea. That he should go."

"But he left before he even said hello to me?"

"That's because he saw you with some artsy-lookin' guy—"

"But—"

"And that's when he just ran for cover. He figured you were toying with him. That he'd get hurt again."

I was beside myself. I could feel my heart beating over his words. "But that guy, that was nothing, you don't understand . . ."

Tom's cell phone rang and he looked at me apologetically and answered it.

I could see how uncomfortable he was and realized how inappropriate this was all getting. Tom and I had gotten along brilliantly when Jack and I were together but we never . . .

"I'm sorry," he said.

"No, it's okay. I'm sorry. You don't deserve to be dealing with this. I shouldn't be—"

"Don't be silly," he said. "Let me walk you over to your friends. It's on my way back to the office and I need to get over there. That call was—"

"You don't have to explain, Tom, really." I felt so embarrassed, so awkward, so regretful.

"Look, maybe when he gets back, you guys should sit down, talk everything over?"

"Gets back?" I asked.

"Sorry. I thought you knew—"

Knew WHAT? I thought.

"He's in Italy—"

"Italy?" I was shocked. "On vacation?"

"Sort of. A few days after your party he just needed to get away and think things through. Pretty extreme. He took a leave of absence from work, sublet his apartment, he's been gone for what, I don't know, months now?"

"Is he there alone?" I had to ask.

He paused and then, "No, Vivian, he's not," he said apologetically.

"I see."

As we arrived in front of the café, we small-talked it a little while the traffic light was red. I asked him to give my love to Lisa and I thanked him for being a very stand-up guy "back there."

"C'mon." He shushed me. "Hey, how's Omelet? He's the best."

"He's great." I said. "The best."

I gave him a kiss on the check and let him walk away. I so wanted to fill him with info to pass on to Jack but knew I'd regret it. I'd get all insecure and try to remember the way I phrased it all. I just let him walk. That was the right thing.

I phoned Sheryl from outside the café, telling her that I was going to pass on her after-hours debauchery and that I'd see her tomorrow.

"Suit yourself," she said.

And just as I hung up my phone rang . . .

"Hey kiddo." It was Reeve.

"Hi," I said, clearing my throat.

"Is this a good time?"

"As good a time as any," I said.

"Well . . . they passed."

I was filled with disappointment. All this time I was dying to know, "either way" ya know, but actually getting the news, the answer I most feared, I then longed for that time again. The time when it was still fifty–fifty.

"You there?" he asked.

"Yes. I'm just digesting it."

"Look, they're fucking idiots and they should have stuck with the first script. This happens all the time out here. Try not to take it personally. It's not you, it's them."

"I know," I said, crossing the street, desperate to find a cab. "It just sucks!"

"I know," he said. "But I'm crazy about ya, Elaine is crazy about ya, the studio is crazy about ya—"

"I know, Reeve, and thanks, but crazy ain't gonna get me a show."

"Not this season, kiddo. But we'll get back out there next year and go for it again."

"I don't know," I said instinctively. "I don't know if I can go through all this again. It takes a toll—"

"I know, kiddo. Give yourself a little time. You'll want it just as bad, once you recover from the news. Trust me."

"I don't know . . ."

"I do. Listen, sit on this for a bit and give me a call in a few days. I'm coming to New York next month. We'll have dinner."

And with that he was gone, other fish to fry, other clients to call . . . it was as simple and understandable as that.

It was business.

thirty-three

Another two months had passed. Omelet's condition was status quo. I had taped a second audition for Lou Lou at a nearby studio. (Me and about another eight New-York-based brunettes.) They had given me a second set of lines, which I rehearsed, at first, with May and Sophie, but they couldn't maintain a straight face. So I resorted to taking advantage of some of the bells and whistles of my office. Enter: video conferencing and my two coaches on the West Coast. S-w-e-e-t. The second time wasn't exactly a charm but at least I knew what I was in for.

I had begun "dating" if that's what you want to call it although every mediocre minute only made me miss Jack more. "Get out there immediately!" was the sage advice and threatening order of my confidantes after I listed "Larry King" as one of my dearest and newest friends. Sure, I was now sufficiently schooled in the political and social climate of our time but I was, too, developing bedsores on my behind. "I swear to God, Viv, one day you're going to go home and find your freakin' television missing!" May barked over a pitcher of sangria at El Cid's. "If you don't initiate for yourself, I'll sic the girls on you!" she warned. "I swear."

"The girls" were just that. An assortment of pseudo-do-gooders at the office, who, if they knew that I was, well, how shall I put this . . . hell, "desperate" to meet someone, would without a doubt be fixin' to fix me with every son, nephew, cousin in their own and their extended families. My personal life would be the topic du jour at the watercooler. So . . .

"Fine!" I huffed. What choice did I have and besides, I knew they were right. "But just answer me this, okay: Does time heal old wounds or does it make the heart grow fonder!?! Huh? 'Cause that's what I want to know. Damn clichés." With that I left them to ponder. The sangria was getting to my head and the spicy tapas was getting to my stomach. But it was much ado about nothing, thankfully, and without an answer upon my return and a sky-high bar tab, we decided to call it an evening.

Yeah, so anyway, I got out there again. I let my kickboxing instructor fix me up. "But just because he'd make a good sparring partner," I explained the next morning, "does not make him a suitable date!!!"

I next finally caved and had coffee with the semicute struggling-screenwriter-slash-Blockbuster-Video-manager who'd been flirting with me for some time and whose gapped front teeth, I must admit, I found oddly attractive. (I couldn't pretend I wasn't single, renting every Sandra Bullock and Julia Roberts movie in existence, consistently, on a month's worth of Friday and Saturday nights.) But I had an out-of-body experience and had to call it quits when I realized that we had actually talked "cinema" for the entire time. We sounded like two Trekkies at a *Star Trek* convention—not not cool—and I have since gotten digital cable.

Then there was my masseur, yes, my masseur. With the best hands in New York. I was sure there had to be other attributes, no, not just physical, that were equally as strong but when he nearly attacked me with his tongue, quite unexpectedly, while we were on line for a Broadway show of all things, I was outta there, actually making a cool one hundred bucks scalping my ticket to *The Producers* to a very nice gentleman from Detroit.

Did I ever search the super-cyber-highway of love? Yes! Okay? Yes, I did. (Deep breath here.) It actually feels incredible to finally admit it. (It's been a dirty dirty secret for far too long!) But after my first and only face-to-face encounter, let me just say politely, an independent private investigator is a very necessary expense.

After the aforementioned experience, I began to fib to my friends and say that I was socializing when I kinda really wasn't. But I did manage, when it was all said and done, to deliver my second finished, edited and all, manuscript right on time. Early, in fact (only because I was given three gracious extensions). So at least there was a plus side.

Lisa and I began to correspond a little, too. A bit after I ran into Tom, she sent me an e-mail, which I returned with a phone call and, supernaturally, I didn't mention Jack at all. She really wanted to get together but I was hesitant. Besides cutting out pasta of all kinds, I got the Jack talk down to a manageable minimum. I would only open up to Omelet, confessing my true feelings from time to time.

Life as I began to know it got easier with each day. Helping May clean out her closets and store some of her things, as she and Daniel had recently cohabitated, was a bit bruising, I'll admit it, but at least the two of them made sense to me, and Daniel always invited me over come award-show time. Sophie and Rob were more of a private "alone time" couple. And I had to conduct an inner conference with myself each time she used that as an excuse not to "play" with me. I wanted to correct her, as in *alone-all-the-time* couple, but I didn't dare.

The only friction at work was the album. It was being held up by record-company corporate bullshit and there was talk that it might be shelved permanently due to the downhill spiral of the music in-

dustry in general. Something about not wanting to take risks pro-
moting, releasing, distributing an album that wasn't guaranteed to
make them a wild fortune right out of the gate. Blah, blah, blah.

"It's not over till it's over." Hawk said in a briefing, but I was so reminded of Reeve at that point that I wasn't counting on it. "Look,
gang, it's business," he went on. "I'm sure that when things perk up,
we'll get back the support we need to make it happen."

The other problem, which he failed to mention, which I knew
wasn't his fault, was that contractually we couldn't shop the album
or the concept anywhere else. The record company owned it plain
and simple. Like your parents' car that's parked in the driveway just
when you get your license, that you're just "not allowed to drive."
No questions asked. Only in this case, pouting got me nowhere.

Wilted, a bunch of us congregated in my office after the record
meeting was adjourned. Sheryl and Drew sharing a cigarette out my
window, Marni, Daniel, and Jayden making room around my desk.
May on my lap. Us all trying to find the bright side.

The only thing any of us knew for certain was that when something flopped, another opportunity always knocked. It was strange
that way. And it wasn't like we would get cocky and sit by the
phones and wait for someone or something interesting to be proposed, but for years, it had always worked that way. And we were
lucky to have that luxury to keep our disappointments company.

"So what next?" I peeped, quite uncharacteristically. I think not
having a novel to write looming over me like a dark cloud, I was itching for something big to do. (Book 3 wouldn't be due for more than
a year.)

"Next? You say it like it's over. Like the record will never see the
light of day," Jayden said.

"Sorry. I didn't mean to . . . I'm just trying to be patient and hopeful. I'm starting to get the feeling that nothing is ever a done deal
until, well, it's done, I guess."

"The less we fret over it, the faster it will resurface. That's my take
anyway," May said.

"You're just probably relieved, little Ms. Heartbreaker," Sheryl teased.

"Don't even go there, Sheryl," I warned.

"Well," Sheryl pointed out, "we've got the second book tour to plan—"

"But it's so early," Marni mentioned.

"It's never too early," Sheryl ripped.

"And then there's the Supreme thing," May added.

"Yeah, but that's basically wrapped," Drew said.

"I don't know about you guys but I think a round of pool is in order," Daniel offered, and we totally agreed. Within minutes we were all gathering our things, off to Luvas, our St. Elmo's if you will, that I hadn't stepped foot into since I'd left for L.A.

As we all waited in the lobby for the elevators, Stan stepped out from his office. "What's this?" he asked rather cheerfully, "a mass exodus?"

"No, not yet," May whispered.

"Hang on," Stan demanded politely. "I need to see you all in the conference room . . . now."

See, what I'd tell ya . . .

thirty-four

Because I would thoroughly understand if you thought that what I'm about to tell you is complete and total fantasy, I feel the need to step outside the realm of fiction at this point and assure you that this all really did take place . . .

Crowded inside the conference room, with our bags packed and our coats on, we all waited anxiously for Stan to unload what was responsible for the giant smile on his face.

"First of all, I want to tell you how proud I am of each of you in this room—"

Sitting next to me, May nudged me with her elbow.

"—and I know how frustrating and disappointing it is when things don't pan out but, as I often say, you cannot ever stop trying." He took a sip of his Evian as though it were Supreme Vodka. "It's always been my feeling that the key to a successful concept, a successful business, is to never give up."

We all shook our heads accordingly, wondering where he was going . . .

"And I need to preface that, again, what I am about to tell you, is absolutely just another, at this stage, incredible but still very get-table opportunity."

We all darted looks of bewildered enthusiasm at each other.

"Polish Publishing was here this morning."

(Polish Publishing was a huge international publishing company responsible for some of the most successful lifestyle, fashion, design, and educational magazines worldwide.)

I grabbed May's hand under the table.

"They are interested in developing a lifestyle magazine called Vivianlives."

We all started screaming, the girls anyway. The guys shared double-fisted hugs and high-fives.

"Now, hang on, hang on," he pleaded, trying to settle us down. "It's just a blueprint. They want to hear our ideas. See a mocked-up version. Listen to our vision."

Sheryl raised her hand like a front-row honor student.

"Yes Sheryl," Stan said, welcoming her question.

"What kind of magazine, Stan? And how much time do we have?"

"Very good questions," he said. "They used the term lifestyle. They want fashion, they want interior, they want recipes, advice, celebrity banter . . ."

I started tearing up. This was such a dream. Just this meeting even. It felt so bizarre yet so understandable. A magazine? Of course! Beyond my wildest expectations—but so not, ya know?

Drew, seated across from me, winked and smiled and nodded at me. I was so happy that we'd never taken it there, you know. It was great to have him on my side for all the right reasons and I so looked forward to working with him on this.

"We've got a month to put it together," Stan said. "And this is what I'm thinking . . . I want to hear your ideas, all of your ideas, or-ganically. What I mean is that I don't want them to come from an overcaffeinated all-night brainstorming session. Individually, I want you to take a few days, independent from each other, and explain what you see to me. Nothing fancy. Just an outline. We'll reconvene in three days once I've reviewed them and strung together the similar themes and highlighted some of the concepts that turn me on. No rules. Think out of the box and, listen, it's not to get out there for public consumption. I was told in no uncertain terms that if this concept shows up in the trades, on a gossip page, if they get so much as a phone call for a comment, anything, it's over. Got me?"

"YES," we all responded.

"Okay, then . . . that's it." He dismissed us. As we all pushed out from our seats and threw our bags over our shoulders, ideas running, racing through our minds, Stan added . . .

"Oh, and Vivian . . ."

"Yes?" I turned to him.

"Congratulations."

I smiled as Jayden came over and put her hand on my shoulder, with May holding my hand, and said, "Thank you."

That was my first ever real Hallmark moment with Stan. I'll never forget it.

Talk about a peace offering.

thirty-five

Luvas was nixed. We were all sufficiently blown away and needed to take comfort, I assumed, within the confines of our own imaginations. Take hold of our expectations, find solitude somewhere, and get thinking. Beyond the obvious, what was also so brilliant about the magazine project was that, finally, Stan saw the value in everyone's take. From mine to those of Jayden and Marni. It wasn't about titles and experience. It was about energy and enthusiasm and teamwork. I could only think that he finally saw our value as a group after what we'd accomplished thus far, and that alone gave me a good feeling that this really could just happen. It had such a pure foundation, right out of the gates.

I remember passing a newsstand as I walked over to the subway, and of course I nearly imploded with pride at just the thought . . .

And I couldn't believe how far we had come. From just a little concept. I thought about the hundreds of meetings I'd taken over the years. The proposals I'd written. The answers I'd given. The dancing. The risks. Yearning for and then earning a solid reputation in an industry oversaturated with mythical ideas, exploited business models, robbed shareholders, disgruntled investors, cynical observers. Fine. So we didn't all make our millions over a Pet Rock or an *I-can't-believe-I-didn't-think-of-it-first* invention. But what we did do, no matter what, was prove that our idea was a good one. Create a brand based on the natural whims of an average girl and leverage it. What would happen next was out of all of our hands. All we could do was our best. And then pray, of course.

I've said it before and I'll say it again: I was raised to be a good person, get a good education, make someone a good wife, and raise a few good children. And maybe hold down a decent job in between. I was raised to think practically. Dreams that seemed far-fetched were just that and it took forever for me to be honest with myself and take a chance and, if it was in my cards, fail. Or maybe not.

Vivianlives was my maybe not.

I live in New York City, I make my own money, explore every whim that I choose to when one floats through my thoughts day to day, week to week, month to month, year to year. And I know now that anything really is possible. And at the same time, I know enough now to understand that some things are not. Possible, that is. For whatever the reason. Just because we want something more than anything else in the world doesn't mean it's going to happen, no matter how much we put into it. And that's why I know above all else how important it is to want it all. It's not selfish, it's vital. Want the love, want the family, want the career. Want the whole pie.

As women, it's unnatural to think that just one area, one accomplishment, is going to bring us the happiness and self-calm that we crave. Nope. It's not like that. We're too complicated and emotional and passionate and fierce.

My point is, follow your heart, every single inch of it. And no matter who tells you different, that's the only way to go. Then there's no second place.

That's what I felt that night. I was already a winner 'cause I was trying. I let myself feel how anyone would if her hard work was acknowledged. I imagined that every other benchmark in my life down the road would fill me with the same undiluted comfort as this latest prospect. Maybe even better, and that's when I couldn't wait another second to let the rest rip!

I didn't dare tell a soul about the magazine. I knew it was too risky. Even though every bit of me wanted to. I rode the train home in much the same way Diane Lane did in *Unfaithful* after she beds up with Olivier Martinez, the first time. (Do you remember that scene? Genius!!!) I couldn't sit still. Giggling, biting my lip, with sheer delight reflecting on that meeting and of what *might* happen.

I remember stepping off the train at my stop and practically skipping home. So eager to hug the hell out of Omelet and share my happiness with him. See, although I knew he might not understand what a magazine was, bear with me here, I was positive that he always knew how I was feeling and would share each emotion with me. It sucked for him that I was a basket case, that's true. Because when I was sad, I knew he was, too, but this, this feeling, I just wanted to pass on to him.

I stopped at the market and picked up a pack of Thomas's English Muffins. I work best when I have a plethora of nooked and crannied toasted muffins spread thick with melted peanut butter at my side. I also got half a pound of Genoa salami for Omelet, a pint of Ben & Jerry's Half Baked frozen yogurt, and a small bouquet of multicolored roses for a little ambience. (I planned on working through the night.)

As I got closer to my apartment, my cell phone rang and I put down my packages in order to answer it.

"Vivian?" the voice asked.

"Yes," I said, not recognizing the voice on the other end.

"It's Lisa!"

"Hey!" I said. "How are you?"

"I'm fine. How are you?"

"I'm great," I answered. "I'm pretty great actually."

"That's nice to hear," she said.

It was great to talk to her. She was such a cool girl. I began to think that a friendship with her might actually be possible. Despite Tom, and despite Jack.

"I'm on my way home," I said. "Just about to walk in."

"Do you want to call me back later?" she asked.

"No, no, it's fine. The only good thing about not living in an elevator building is that I'm guaranteed cell phone service. You know what?" I went on, "it's turning out to be a nice night. Let me just sit down here and talk to you for a bit. How are you feeling?"

I sat on my steps for the next fifteen minutes, catching up with her. This conversation was much less guarded than our previous one. She and Tom were coming up with names for the baby; she was designing earrings from home, selling them to a few small shops near her apartment. She sounded great.

I told her about Omelet, about Sophie, about May. "Jesus," she exhaled. "It's been some year for you, hasn't it?"

"Yeah, but I'm finding the silver lining," I assured her.

"You've got to."

"So much for the nice night," I said, noting the drops of rain that were falling on me much like confectioners' sugar.

"It's already raining here," she said—that would be Brooklyn.

We stayed on the line as I made my way inside and upstairs. As I fumbled for my keys, she raised the Jack topic.

"I haven't seen Jack . . . since he's been back."

I stopped looking for my keys and stood frozen outside my door. "Viv?"

"Yeah, I'm here. He's back, huh?"

"Uh-huh. A few days ago. Tom doesn't think I should meddle but—"

"Lisa . . ."

"I know, I know." She hesitated. "Do you still—"

"YES," I said before I even knew what she was going to ask.

"I knew it," she cried, delighted.

My two neighbors passed me as I stood outside my door. "Are you locked out?" one said.

"No, I'm okay. Thanks." I found my keys.

"Were you talking to me?" she asked.

"No, my neighbors."

"The dueling queens?" she remembered.

"Yup," I said. "I'm standing outside my apartment like a freak. Hang on a second." I reached for my keys and opened the door, still yapping. Once inside, I placed my things down at the entryway table and grabbed the Ben & Jerry's to put in the freezer.

I remember Lisa asking me for plans. That we needed to hang out. She wanted me to help her decorate her baby's room. But that's about it. When I walked out of the kitchen I saw Omelet on his back on the carpet in my living room. He was convulsing, barely able to breathe. His eyes and nose were gray and he didn't hear or see me. I dropped the phone and fell to my knees. Screaming his name, petting his head. He was soaking wet, sweating. I yelled for help over and over again and ran for the phone. I dialed 911, my hands and fingers trembling so much that I actually dialed 9-1-4 and then 9-9-1 the first two times.

My dueling neighbors rushed in and helped me carry Omelet down the street to our vet.

Remembering now, it's really all a blur. We didn't wait for traffic lights; we didn't get out of the way for anyone on the street. We burst into the vet's office and they rushed Omelet into an examining room, forcing me to wait outside.

The only word I could find, all that time, from the moment I saw him on my living room floor until I sat under the fluorescent lights in a private room at the vet's was Omelet.

I cried and cried. That headache kind of cry. Where your eyeballs get sore and your tears actually possess weight. How long had he been lying there suffering? Would I ever see him again?

My dueling neighbors went back to my apartment and fetched

my handbag and my coat. They returned with a cup of coffee and asked if I needed anything. I was so touched by their kindness.

The vet on duty, Dr. Fries, came in and sat next to me. "He's hanging in there, Vivian," he said. "He had a stroke and he's going to need to stay here tonight so we can observe him."

I held his hand tightly. "Is he . . ." I couldn't finish my sentence. I couldn't catch my breath.

"He's sleeping now. We pumped him full of meds so I can tell you for sure that he's not in any pain. But we'll need to wait and see what kind of irrevocable damage he's suffered and then you'll need to decide—"

"How did this happen?"

"Omelet has cancer, Vivian, and although he has been doing well since he's been on the cortisone, you can never be certain what changes will take place day after day. There's nothing that you could have done or I could have done to prevent this. Let's just wait and see, okay?"

"Can I see him?" I pleaded.

"In a little bit," he conceded. "Do you want us to call anyone for you?" he asked kindly.

"Yes," I said. "Sophie. My friend. Her number is on that 'in case of emergency' paperwork you guys have us fill out."

"Okay. I'll have Lydia do that now."

"Thank you," I sniffled.

"You can stay here as long as you like. And there's a vending machine out in the lobby if you need anything."

"Thank you, Doctor Fries."

"You're welcome."

thirty-six

I waited in what felt like solitary confinement for just about an hour. I was in a straitjacket of my very own. I couldn't move. I couldn't help. I couldn't be there for my sweet companion. Whenever I started to calm down, the very next instant I'd work myself up into a frenzy again, realizing how much my tears tranquilized me. The calm was too scary, too much of what my life would be like without Omelet in it. So it felt better to cry.

Lydia, the gentle office manager, came in to check on me. I was still on my own and she was concerned. I asked if it would be okay if I called my family; my cell phone, I gathered, was still on my floor where I'd dropped it.

"Of course." She brought me to her office. "Omelet is stabilizing, sweetie," she offered. "He doesn't feel a thing."

"I know. Thank you, Lydia."

"I'm just outside if you need anything."

I smiled and called my parents. As the phone rang I looked over Lydia's desk. There were small framed pictures of half a dozen cats and dogs. It was comforting to know that she understood how much I could love him.

When my mother picked up I lost it again. My dad got on the line from a second phone and they tried to console me. They offered to drive in but it was late and I was holding on to Dr. Fries's words of optimism. That's when Sophie, along with Rob and Lydia, entered.

She was in tears, her face swollen. She just hugged me. My parents were relieved to know that I wasn't alone and said that they would get in touch with Joseph and have him meet me there. Rob offered his sympathies and asked if he could get me anything. His kindness, too, was duly noted.

Dr. Fries emerged, saying it was all right to go in and see Omelet. I wouldn't be able to touch him or get too close, but at least I could see where he was and know that he was in good hands.

Sophie offered to join me but I felt that I needed to go alone. It wasn't a dramatic notion but instead an instinctual one. I entered a new, larger room. White but for the blue linens and chrome apparatus. I thought about how sterile and strange the space felt. Not a homey vibe in sight.

Omelet looked peaceful. Out of harm's way. I knew it was an illusion, but it was an image I needed to create in order to leave him there. Dr. Fries whisked me in as quickly as he whisked me out and when we returned to Lydia's office, he asked if we could have a moment alone. Sophie and Rob said they would wait for me in the lobby.

"I need you to read this over," he said, handing me what looked like a one-page affidavit-slash-contract.

"What is it?" I asked.

"It's a document that authorizes me and my staff to, well, should Omelet suffer any kind of unexpected complications during the night, we can use our best judgment . . ."

I was shocked. As if someone had just sucker punched me. "But I thought you said—"

"Vivian, Omelet is very ill, and every animal is different. Every situation is unique. I'm not saying that anything will happen, but we will be monitoring him all night and . . ."

I took a deep breath and grabbed a pen from Lydia's desk. I signed my name as tears again began to stray from my sore eyes. They were lighter this time, falling swiftly. As if the reality had settled and the cancer had won.

I handed him back the document and sat up straight, trying as hard as I could do be rational and responsible, putting my emotions on hold. "Please, Doctor Fries. I trust you to use your best judgment. I don't want Omelet to suffer because I need him, you know?"

"Yes. We will. And I understand, completely."

I met Sophie and Rob out front. I thanked Lydia and was about to exit the office, but I was afraid to. I didn't want to leave him there. Alone. I began to feel faint and sat back down again. And the tears just kept coming.

Rob left to get the car. He was going to pull up right out front, and Sophie thought it would be a good idea if we picked up a pizza or something. Rob would drop us off at my apartment, and Sophie told me she'd sleep over.

I was stuck inside myself. While feeling so sad and hopeless, I felt overly dramatic, wanting so hard to be stronger than "this," ya know. I was completely uncomfortable feeling so exposed and open. I wanted to deal and grieve privately but I couldn't hold it in. Looking back, I think fighting it every step of the way just made it worse.

"Vivian," Sophie whispered. "Omelet will be here when we come back tomorrow, honey. He will. I know it. Come on. We've got to go."

But I just couldn't get up. I was terrified that this would be the last night and I thought somehow if I stayed still I could freeze time. Prolong it. Ensuring that morning would just blend right in and everything would be back to normal.

"I spoke to Joseph," she said. "He's on his way to your apartment. We'll all stay with you and we'll come back with salami and treats for Omelet in the morning. Come on now, sweetie. Let's go."

I knew she was thinking clearly. So I sat up and held her hand and walked out into the cold night. The rain had let up, but the sound of the watered-down streets and cars gliding through the pockets of puddles had a loneliness that only I could hear.

I got into the back of Rob's Jeep and Sophie closed the door behind me. She got in and awkwardly suggested Pinsone's, a favorite pizza place just down the block. It was so close, in fact, that Rob just put the car in park and confirmed, "Pepperoni?"

To which Sophie replied, "Yup. And get it well done, baby."

"Gotcha," he said and disappeared.

For a fleeting moment I could see what Sophie saw in him. He seemed genuine and kind and gentle, having left all the trappings that I'd first encountered behind.

"Thank you, Sophie," I said.

"Awww, Vivi," she said, turning to me in the back, "everything is going to be okay. You won't go through this alone." She turned back around and dialed her cell phone, speaking to Joseph who was apparently already at my apartment. I could tell the serious nature of his questions based solely on the brief protective yes and no answers she was giving him.

Instead of doing my best to eavesdrop, I sat back and turned my face toward the vet's office. I leaned my forehead against the window and stared out solemnly. My breath began to fog up my view so I pulled down the right sleeve of my blouse and began to wipe the window off.

With a new clear view I saw a man's silhouette try to enter the vet's office. He pulled the door a few times, and when he realized it was locked he began pounding on it. I could make out Lydia as she walked toward the man. As the glass again began to fog up, I rubbed it with my bare hand. The cold sensation ran through my palm, down my arm, and enveloped my chest. With a clear view, I could see them, still talking. Lydia, round, short, in a white top and teal cardigan sweater, white pants, and white shoes. The man, tall, in a skullcap, blackened trench, baggy denim jeans, and gray sneakers.

I focused in. I could make out the cream-colored floor and even see a small shiny blue crumbled bag of potato chips that looked as if it had fallen accidentally from a purse or a pocket and lingered, practically hidden, in the corner by the door. I could see Lydia's white shoes begin to move away and then I saw the gray sneakers turn as they walked out.

In a moment, the kind of moment that seems timeless but in actuality only exists for a split second, I remembered the day we first— well, the day we second—met. Jack. It was at the firehouse, which Omelet and I visited with the hope of thanking, personally, the man who'd saved Omelet from a fire in the apartment Sophie and I had shared, years ago. I remembered Omelet greeting a then stranger, in the way that only Omelet could, with a smothering onslaught of devotion. The man crouching down, responding and almost defending himself from this affection-filled animal. Camouflaged in white fur, my first glimpse of our hero was his sneakers. Gray-silver old-school New Balance.

I grabbed hold of that memory, of Jack, of Omelet and the day that changed me forever. When Jack entered our lives and how happy we were. I leaned my forehead again onto the cold car window and watched as it began to fog over. I felt the tears coming but thankfully they were happier ones. A bittersweet memory that I knew would remain vivid in my mind's eye for eternity.

For a third time, I sat up and wiped the window clear. I wanted to conjure up another memory, something gentle and eloquent, something that could comfort me. And when I opened my eyes, there was Jack again, still our hero, staring back at me with a smile so warm that it sang its own lullaby.

It took another timeless moment, one of those forever split seconds, for me to realize that I wasn't dreaming this time.

epilogue

My first thought: Where to begin? (Pretty funny considering this is the epilogue.)

Lydia had called Jack after she'd left Sophie a message that night. (He was on my emergency call sheet, too.) I spent seconds just staring at his image, losing myself in what I assumed was another wild hallucination. It was not until he put his hand on my window that I allowed myself to think and hope that it was actually him. Flesh and blood. I'll never forget our first embrace. Ever.

After a short while, Sophie and Joseph happily left Jack and I and a few pieces of pizza in my apartment. We stayed up all night. Talking, explaining, apologizing, comforting each other. Grief-stricken, and in his arms, it was the only place I could ever have been.

In fact, Jack and I are doing great. I say "I love you" every chance I get and have officially started fantasizing about the day, whenever it is, that we make it official. There's no rush, of course, but it's very nice to no longer think of my wedding day as the finale of a horror movie. So, I'm making progress.

Omelet floated up to heaven three weeks later. We had a beautiful ceremony and I sprinkled his ashes in a lovely spot along the Hudson River in upstate New York where he used to love to play. My parents, Joseph, Jack, and Sophie were in attendance.

I miss him all the time. I wear my pendant every day and each time I feel it graze along my chest it comforts me dearly. And I'm still—and I'm sure will forever be—profoundly touched by how much joy and comfort a single creature could give me. Life goes on, of course, but I know that Omelet made my life that much sweeter.

Work is, well, just that. The ups and downs are exciting and all but I've been thinking about taking a break. Maybe some time off, we'll see. I'm just frustrated. The record is still chillin' atop a "maybe" pile at some record executive's office and I'm seriously thinking about organizing a covert mission to rescue it and find it a new home. My magazine? Oh my God, don't even get me started. Polish Publishing went and lost millions in a dispute over one of their failed titles, just weeks after we presented our demo and received a standing ovation and contracts the following afternoon. So again, shocker, we're on "hold"—no new business, blah, blah, blah. Cruel. I was passed over for the movie role but that was the least of my disappointments. I've just finished a second pilot script for television that I love and, well, everything is moving along. And yes, I know, it's great that these opportunities keep coming—I was in the meeting, remember? But I'm starting to understand why people fall off the deep end. All I can say is, thank God for these novels!!! They keep me (half) sane. At the very least, they force me to relive and learn from each of my experiences and make me laugh realizing how crazy life can get. I just want to keep growing, trying my hand at new things, feeling the rush. I like living on the edge. My little edge. I'm sure I'd get bored if things were any different. Well, maybe not, but it sounds better than giving in to disillusionment!

Sophie and Rob are getting married at the end of the summer. A big Hamptons gala affair and if there was ever a girl who could be the belle of the ball it's our little Sophie for sure! She's even thinking about starting her own wedding planning business . . . thankfully, the talk of her moving to Los Angeles with Rob was just that, talk. They're staying put and *relieved* ain't even the word!

Daniel and May are doing well and are still "Smitten" in more ways than one. Jayden and the bartender from my book launch party have broken up and gotten back together more times than I can count, and Marni just left on maternity leave.

Sheryl hasn't given up her fighting spirit but she has given up on that yoga boy. Evidently his schedule wasn't as flexible as his limbs and, not feeling like a priority, Sheryl, the woman who never settles, has since moved on. A tough cookie, that one. She and Stan, of all people, have been working a lot of late nights, on what I'm not sure exactly, and I'm just days away of getting to the bottom of it! So weird!

Drew is now officially single, sort of. He and Butt broke up and now he's dating a new and I think the first-ever female account executive at Supreme Vodka. I count him as one of my dearest friends.

Tom and Lisa had a beautiful baby girl, Eva, and Jack and I both stood up for them at their wedding, in Las Vegas, a few months back.

Joseph has moved back to New York (city) and I love having him here. He adopted a dog right after he decided on a permanent residence and after seeing how much attention his nephew got him! He's still searching for the perfect "chick" and I'm still trying to figure out what is wrong with him!!!

My parents are doing well. My dad was "incentivized" to retire early. He's a bit upset and offended but he's enjoying his leisure time. He's used it quite wisely actually, sending me a handmade brochure of the best plastic surgeons in the tri-state area and a blank check, still hoping that I lose the ink. (Jack digs it by the way. "Hot," he says but never dares to incorporate the word "stripper.") They (parents) finally ordered cable television and are deliriously happy that Jack and I got back together. My mom sends him a frozen vegetarian lasagna on the first Thursday of every month, and she, after one too many glasses of wine, told Jack to call her "mom" at a recent dinner. I almost died.

Jack's family is still a bit icy toward me but I understand. I'm confident they'll come around at some point. Gina, I'm not too sure about, but you've got to believe!

Jack is thinking of leaving the fire department for good. He's been flirting with the idea of opening up a restaurant. I just watch in the wings and cross my fingers that whatever he wants, whatever he thinks will make him happy, actually does. Honestly you guys, I'm becoming such a good girlfriend I almost want to date myself!

Perhaps there are a few exceptions to the zebra rule!

Anyway, I just want to thank you for everything. I hate goodbyes. I usually let my phone go to voice-mail or I arrive way too late to get poignant, but when you write these books there's no getting out of it. . . .

Short and sweet this time: It's been a privilege and a pleasure and I'll always be rooting for you just as you have done for me.

Until we meet again and with all my love,

ViViAN ☺

About the Authors

Bronx born, SHERRIE KRANTZ grew up in New York and attended the University of Buffalo. She spent the first leg of her career as a public relations executive, first at Calvin Klein, Inc., and then at Donna Karan International. From there, Sherrie founded Forever After, Inc., parent company to *www.Vivianlives.com*, and cowrote *The Autobiography of Vivian: A Novel* and *Vivian Lives*. She continues to develop projects for television, film, and print and enjoys the company of her forever-puppy, Stella. She resides in New York City.

VIVIAN LIVINGSTON is a bit of an enigma. Although she hasn't given up her NYC apartment, rumor has it that she has outgrown her Dorothy-esque ways and is now traveling abroad with a certain someone. . . . Whereabouts unknown, she has alluded to a "next, new" manuscript, the contents of which still remain to be seen. Hmmmmmmmmm.